To the woman I once was, you've done it. Even when you thought you couldn't, you did it. Through the ups and the downs, you stuck through it. I'm proud of you. Keep going, and never give up. You can do anything you put your mind to.

And to those who helped me along the way, I couldn't have done it without you. You've helped me realize my potential and pushed me to do something I never thought I could. You've believed in me even when I didn't believe in myself. You are all such amazing people, and I appreciate everything you have done for me.

And lastly, to those who didn't believe in me. Guess what? I did it. I fucking did it, and I'm going to keep doing it – just watch me.

# Contents

# Content Warnings

- Sexual content

- Physical and emotional abuse

- Domestic violence

- Child abuse

- Mention of suicide

- Mention of sexual assault

- Voyeurism

- Light BDSM

- Attempted kidnapping

- Mentioned kidnapping

- Cliffhanger

- Growing harem throughout series

# Pronunciation Guide

## Characters

- Ahmeira – Ah-meer-uh

- Amaroc – Am-uh-rock

- Ambrose – Am-brr-ohz

- Anevae – Ana-vay

- Calliope – Cuh-lie-oh-pee

- Casimir – Cah-suh-meer

- Cordilaen – Core-duh-lane

- Eirian – Eye-ree-an

- Eiri – Eye-ree

- Emrhys – Em-reese

- Maeyve – May-v

- Roarc – Row-arc

- Tanith – Tah-nith

*Places*

- Baeruil – Bay-roo-ill

- Caellaias – Kah-lay-us

- Ceraias – Sir-A-us

- Eirvanna – Air-Vanna

- Kaeuil – Kay-U-ill

- Kanlyrae – Can-luh-ray

- Kolathus – Coal-ah-TH-us

- Lamatorre – La-muh-tore

- Maiviraea – My-vuh-ray-uh

- Rilias – Rih-lie-us

- Rilvara – Ril-var-uh

### *Other*

- Nyrthym – Near-thim

- Orletaylaer – Or-leh-tay-lair

- Sollamthus – Sol-am-thus

- Zyelvris – ZIE-el-vr-iss

# The Calling of Caellaias

## Book One of The Kingdom of Caellaias Series

### Mikaelynn Rose

# Prologue

As a little girl, I was captivated by the strange lands Momma always talked about. Eiri, born just two years after me, always wanted to be anywhere I was. I was her big sister, Vayvay, as she called me then. We enjoyed hearing everything Momma was willing to share with us; even though we may not have understood it all at the time, we loved it nonetheless.

Poppa insisted Momma shouldn't tell them to us, which often caused them to argue when Eiri and I went to bed. He told us that Momma's stories were just fairytales. We didn't care if the stories were real; we soaked up every opportunity to hear them. Every time Momma would call for us, Eiri and I would sit on the floor, ready to hear Momma's silky-smooth voice tell us one of her many stories. We always loved hearing them, even if it upset Poppa.

According to her stories, the kingdom of Caellaias was a mesmerizing land with periwinkle skies and white fluffy clouds. In the dark night sky, a bright purple moon would sparkle like glitter. The rich and diverse landscape extended as far as the eye could see, and the Kolathus mountains reached high into the sky with snow-covered peaks. An abundance of trees called zyelvris trees spread throughout the land, encased in mahogany bark and decorated with red leaves. Rumor has it that when the trees shed their leaves, they shift from red to purple and give off the scent of marshmallows. During the late season, they would ooze sap that tasted of butter.

Frequent rainfall made the lush, deep green grasses fragrant. Just as in our world, Caellaias had a variety of flowers and plants in an assortment of vibrant colors. When the flowers bloomed in large concentrations, their fragrances could be detected even a couple of miles away. Momma frequently talked about the orletaylaer—a bright teal rose-like flower—which was her favorite in all of Caellaias.

Her gaze became unfocused when she spoke about the faraway kingdom, and longing danced behind her brilliant silver eyes. It was almost as if she were recalling a memory, not a fairytale. But if Poppa was correct, the world wasn't real; it was only a figment of Momma's imagination.

One afternoon, while Poppa was at work, Momma came to find Eiri and me playing in my room. She invited us to the living room to tell us one of her stories. Since Poppa was at work, she was free to speak about Caellaias without fear of upsetting him. We followed her to the couch, settling on the floor before her.

Before she began, she leaned forward and kissed my head. "Alright, my Little Lily." Then, she turned to Eiri and did the same. "And my Little Rose." These weren't our proper names but nicknames our parents had given us. At times, when they addressed the both of us together, they called us their Flowers.

"It's story time. What kind of story would you like to hear today?" Momma asked as she sat on the couch, feet folded below her long skirt.

"I want to hear all about Caellaias again!" I exclaimed.

As Momma looked at me, her silver eyes gleamed.

"I've told you some about Caellaias, but have I ever told you about the different territories?" She asked, already knowing the answer.

"No! Please tell us," Eiri begged.

"Well, at the center of the kingdom is Eirvanna. Once considered the land of the faeries, it's now home to a vast number of beings. The lands surrounding it cause a cyclical change of weather patterns, making it suitable for many different beings."

"In the northern part of the kingdom is a place called Maiviraea. It is the land of the shifters –"

"Momma," I interrupted.

She patiently glanced down at me. "Yes, my Lily?"

"What's a shifter?" I asked.

"Shifters are beings that can turn into an animal."

"What kind of animal?" Eiri asked with excitement.

"It depends on the person, but there are many, *many* types. In order for all these different types of shifters to feel at home, the land has every kind of habitat imaginable. It's as though, within Maiviraea's borders, a miniature version of Caellaias exists.

"The western part of Maiviraea is the warmest, all sand and scorching heat like a desert. Some animals you may find there are camels, ginormous scorpions, and various types of reptiles. The easternmost part is mountainous, as the Kolathus mountains run from Eirvanna to the ocean. The further east you go, it becomes bitter cold, with frequent snowfalls and blizzards. This area is home to bears, mountain goats, and rabbits. In the north, it's very humid as it borders the ocean. Many of the animals from this area come from the ocean, such as seals, penguins, and turtles. The southern piece is the furthest inland and full of trees. Deer, wolves, foxes, and other woodland animals live there."

Momma shifted to look out the window at the snow falling outside. "To the east of Eirvanna is Baeruil, which is the home of the angels. The ground is always covered in snow, and the sun *always* shines. According to the angels who live there, it's like living on a cloud, so peaceful and calm because few other beings live there."

Momma refocused on us as she continued, "If you travel south of Eirvanna, you'll find yourself in Lamatorre—the home of the vampires. Because of a special spell, the sun can't shine fully, making plant life sparse. There are occasional patches of grass or flowers, and most of the trees are all hollowed out and dead. It's truly a dreadful place, but it's perfect for the vampires; their eyes and skin are very sensitive to the sun."

"I'm glad I'm not a vampire!" Eiri interrupted, "I love being outside in the sun!"

Chuckling, Momma continued, "To the west of Eirvanna is the land of the demons called Kaeuil. Similar to Lamatorre, it is also barren. However, the sun relentlessly beats down on the land here, causing it to be constantly hot and dry. It's exactly what many people in the Earth realm think of Hell. The land is so hot it's uninhabitable for many beings.

"But my favorite place in *all* of Caellaias is Castle Rilvara! It's a beautiful white stone castle nestled on the edge of the forest in Eirvanna, home to the royal family along with their hundreds of guards and servants.

"The castle has four looming spires that reach high up into the sky like they are trying to touch the clouds. These spires are tipped with a brilliant cobalt-blue stone called sollamthus. The gray walls protecting the castle stand over one hundred feet tall, and sitting atop them are what they call battlements. The walls barricade the castle from the dangers of the forest and any enemies who dare to attack those living there; archers and guards defend the castle from the battlements. If an enemy avoids being hit by an arrow, they have to cross a moat full of piranha-like fish called nyrthym to reach the wall itself.

"On the opposite side of the forest is the city of Kanlyrae. Hundreds of people reside there and are frequently visited by tourists and travelers on their way from one territory to another. Traveling merchants come from all over to display and trade their wares. Farmers from the outskirts of the city set up produce and meat stands," Momma explained.

"Momma, I wish we could visit Caellaias one day! It sounds *so* magical! I want to taste the zyelvris sap!" I begged, staring at her with wide eyes and a bright smile.

Her eyes met mine, terror evident on her face. She grasped my hand, pulling me into a tight hug. "My Little Lily, I wish we could. It's such a beautiful place but can be very dangerous." As Momma hugged me, her tears dropped onto my shoulder. She took a deep breath before continuing, "The royal family is not all they seem to be. Long ago, the king lived in the castle with his beautiful wife, the queen. They were blessed with two beautiful daughters, just a few years apart.

"Sadly, the queen passed away after she had her second daughter. The king did his best to care for and raise his daughters, but, in the end, they both ran away. You see, the king is easily angered, and his anger makes him cruel. He doesn't think about how he affects others when he lashes out. His subjects adore him very much, but he is not the same man to those closest to him. So, as much as I'd love to take you there, Poppa would never allow it, and if we go, we may never be able to come home."

When Momma finally let me go, I looked up and wiped away another tear from her cheek as I said, "Momma, the princesses sound brave. I want to be brave like them someday," and gave her a small smile.

She returned my smile and nodded. Caressing my cheeks and taking a deep breath, she murmured, "My Little Lily, I have no doubt you will be even more brave than they ever could have been. You can do anything you put your mind to. Now, you girls, go play while I finish supper." With that, she kissed me on the forehead and rushed into the kitchen, sniffling several times along the way.

# Chapter One

## Anevae

As I stepped onto the dirt driveway, the bright early morning sunlight reflected off the windows of the two-story cabin before me. Surrounding the house was a mixture of aspen and pine trees varying in size and shape. The heart-shaped leaves of the aspens were a vibrant green, while the needles of the pines were a deeper shade. The rising sun left the sky above a stunning light shade of orange. Closing my eyes, I inhaled the fresh mountain air and fragrant pines as the sounds of nature encompassed me; crickets chirped, birds sang their harmonious songs, and a soft trickle resounded from a creek in the distance. I was excited to be able to call this stunning place my new home.

Approximately five years earlier, I graduated from Yale, an Ivy League university, at the top of my class. I majored in biological engineering, where I focused mainly on agriculture. After graduation, I was recruited by a prestigious company, Ultra-Precision Agriculture Incorporated. It was a great job where I gained a lot of experience. I excelled in the company, and because of the recognition I'd received, I moved up in the industry quickly. That was the reason for my move.

A Colorado-based company called Vision For The Future approached me with an enticing offer to conduct research from the comfort of my own home. Of course, I had accepted, but that meant I had to find a house suitable for my needs. The cabin before me was perfect; with a greenhouse attached, I had a safe place where I could perform indoor experiments, and of course, the land attached meant I had plenty of space for outdoor experiments as well.

I remained where I stood for a moment, enjoying the peaceful sounds and wondrous scents. The rumbling of a vehicle traveling up the mile-long driveway to my home interrupted my peace. The moving truck my parents rented was here.

My eyes flew open, and I locked my maroon SUV, mainly out of habit since I'd grown up in a big city. Heading toward the front door of my new home, I reached into my coat pocket to retrieve my house keys. I wanted to open the door and prepare for the chaos that would ensue when my family arrived.

After fumbling with the lock momentarily, I nudged the massive door open and took a small step inside. The cabin was built using mahogany wood, and the interior was rich in color. A loud honk startled me, and I headed back outside to join my family.

Walking out the front door, I watched Eirian gracefully climb out of the moving truck with her long, naturally silver hair flowing out behind her. Her striking silver eyes—inherited from our mom—met mine as a smile crested her lips. She wasn't just my sister but also my best friend in the entire world. We had been inseparable from the moment she arrived in the world. We told each other everything, and when I told her I was moving halfway across the country, she insisted on joining me on my new adventure.

Glancing to the other side of the truck, my dad, whom we lovingly called Poppa, hopped down from the driver's seat. His round, electric blue eyes immediately locked onto me, no doubt making sure I was alright. His crimson-colored hair, which I inherited, was short on the sides but long enough on the top that he could slick it back—the way he'd worn it since I was little. His appearance was always immaculate; there was never a hair out of place or a wrinkle in his clothes.

My mom—we called her Momma—closely followed as she inspected the unfamiliar surroundings. Her silver hair was freshly trimmed into the typical short pixie cut she preferred. Like Poppa, she wore blue jeans, a loose gray T-shirt, and navy sneakers, which was unusual for her. Momma always wore dresses or skirts, but it wasn't practical with the move. Seeing her like that was strange but interesting.

My parents stood together near the truck, concern etched on their faces as they continued to peer around. They were worried when I initially told them I was moving halfway across the country to a remote area of the Rocky Mountains in Colorado. Their worry intensified when they learned that Eiri was coming with me. While I had purchased the cabin in the mountains, my sister took a different route and found an apartment in a nearby town, Havenridge. After hours of yelling, screaming, and crying, our parents relented, knowing they couldn't talk us out of our plans. Their primary stipulation was that they would help us with the move so they could make sure the area was safe for us. Unfortunately, our new homes were over a day's drive from our hometown, but our parents didn't seem to mind. Either way, I sincerely appreciated their help with the move and concern for our safety.

"How was the drive up?" I asked as I approached my family. "I hope it wasn't too hard to find your way here. I know GPS doesn't work well in these mountains. I lost signal a couple of times on the way up, but thankfully, I've been here a few times now."

While we made most of the trek to the area together, we had gone our separate ways the day before. My family went to Eiri's apartment in Havenridge to get her situated while I went to Fawnhaven, the big city on the opposite side of my cabin, to meet with my sponsors and retrieve supplies for my experiments. Since I knew I'd be in the city for the majority of the day, I stayed there for the night instead of driving back to Eiri's.

My sister ran up and wrapped me in a big bear hug. After a moment, she took a step back to look around. "You sure picked a beautiful place; it's incredible up here.

"We only saw one other house on our way up. It's wild to think that you only have one neighbor. Who knows if there's even anyone living in the cabin? This is a drastic difference from the big city we're so used to." Pausing, she looked at me with humor dancing in her eyes. "I *also* want to point out that the closest store is *at least* thirty minutes from you. I'm only visiting once a week, tops!  No ifs, ands, or buts!"

I rolled my eyes. "Eiri, you do realize I have a vehicle to get myself around, right? I won't need you to bring me things...*often*," I added with a giggle that quickly evolved into a full-blown laughing fit between us.

My parents chuckled and shook their heads as they strolled up behind Eiri, each taking turns hugging me. They looked exhausted but still insisted on helping with the remainder of the move. The moving truck was also their transport home, so they couldn't leave without it.

"Anevae, this is a gorgeous plot of land indeed. When autumn comes, many of the leaves on the aspen trees will be a beautiful red like in Caellaias. I can't wait to see that..." Momma trailed off as Poppa cleared his throat. She refocused and glanced back at me. "Your Poppa and I are very proud of you, Lily... I know we just got here, but in hopes of finishing before nightfall, shall we get started?" she asked, glancing between the three of us.

With all of us in agreement, I showed my family around the house before we began unpacking the truck. When we packed it at home, Eiri and I separated all our belongings to avoid mixing things up. My boxes had been thoroughly labeled with the area each one should go in to make unloading the truck and unpacking easier. Even though my new place was at least twice the size of my previous apartment, I had taken the initiative to downsize as much as possible to help simplify the move. My new cabin came with all the needed appliances, so I didn't have to worry about those when I moved in either.

After what felt like hours of work, we stopped for lunch. We headed into the kitchen as Momma retrieved the cooler with all our favorites. There were several sandwiches, various cheeses and chips to snack on, multiple bottles of water, and a few cans of soda.

She passed out our lunches and handed each of us a water bottle, insisting that we drink it before we drank any soda to stay hydrated. We dutifully gulped down our water and then quickly ate. After we finished, we set back to work, hoping to finish before it got too dark.

Once we were done bringing in my bedroom set—the last piece of my belongings—we gathered in the living area. Although I was sore from the day of work, my family had to be even more sore. They'd worked hard moving Eiri's belongings the day before, and I knew she didn't downsize in the least. I felt terrible that I couldn't help them with her stuff, but I had to meet with my sponsors.

My family settled in on the couch while I plopped down on the floor in front of them, exhausted; the last few days had been busy for all of us. Even with that, I wanted to spend every possible moment with my parents before they went back home. I knew I'd miss them greatly.

"May I treat you all to dinner as a thank you for your help? Eiri and I couldn't have done this without you. There's a little diner in Havenridge, about a half mile from Eiri's new apartment, that I want to try. It's called Minnie's. If their milkshakes are as good as everyone says, it would be special to visit it with you all first," I said, giving them a pleading look.

My parents exchanged a lengthy glance. This was a common occurrence when faced with a decision that involved them both. It was as if they could communicate telepathically. They married a couple of years before I was born and had been friends for several years before that. They knew everything about each other.

After a few minutes, Poppa answered with his deep, gruff voice, "That sounds wonderful, Lily. Since we won't see you two for a while, one last family meal is needed indeed. Leaving in the morning is going to be difficult." A grin spread across his lips, displaying his pronounced canines and slightly crooked teeth.

"Great! Let me gather my things so we can get going. Eiri, do you want to ride with me so you won't be cramped in the moving truck again?" I asked with a smirk.

"That would be great! I've spent way too much time in that truck over the last few days!" Eiri said, and I chuckled.

She waited on the couch as I headed into the kitchen to retrieve my keys.

# Chapter Two

## *Anevae*

When I returned to the living room, Eiri was still sitting on the couch, but our parents were gone. Eiri barely glanced up from her phone to let me know they had gone outside to get some fresh air and that we could meet them outside when we were ready.

Her attention on her screen made me realize I hadn't checked my phone all day. I pulled it out and scrolled through my notifications. There wasn't anything that couldn't wait until later or the next day.

"You ready?" I asked, shoving my phone back into my pocket.

Eiri nodded and stood to follow me outside. Pushing the key fob, I unlocked my SUV so she could get in, then started it with the click of another button before turning to lock the door to my cabin. When I was done, I climbed into the front seat of my SUV and put the car in drive. My parents followed in the moving truck as we drove to the main road.

"How's the job search going?" I asked.

Before the move, Eiri was an assistant editor for a small publishing company in our hometown. She began working there right after she graduated from college three years earlier.

"I mean, it's going about as well as it can, I guess. Thankfully, Tim, the editor I worked under, was kind enough to contact some of his colleagues to help me find a new job. He secured six interviews for me in the next few weeks. Six! Can you believe it? That's so many! And, like, four of them are work-from-home jobs!"

I smiled at her enthusiasm. "That was very nice of him. He was always such a great guy. Where are the two local positions? Are they both in Havenridge, or would you have to travel to Fawnhaven?"

She began twirling a piece of her hair. "One is in Havenridge, but you know it's such a small town. The other is in Fawnhaven. I don't really want to drive that far, but I'm going to the interview to show my appreciation for Tim's help."

"You said there were four remote positions, too, right? Are you excited about those? I'm sure it would be nice to work from home."

"I'd love to work from home, but you know how I am. I'd probably go crazy if I couldn't talk to someone else constantly, Vay! I'd end up bugging you all the time! Speaking of, how the hell can you even contemplate being out there all by yourself? All that surrounds you in that cabin is nature and the one potential neighbor you have."

Pulling up to the stop light leading into town, I looked at her. "Just because you like people and interacting with them doesn't mean everyone does. I love the idea of being able to work from home. Plus, I'll just get to bug you more often since you're the only person I know who lives nearby." Sticking my tongue out, I returned my gaze to the road.

"Well, I'm glad I can be of some service to someone while I'm out of a job. I'm really not looking forward to organizing and unpacking," Eiri grumbled.

I laughed loudly as we pulled into the diner's parking lot. "Well, that sure sucks for you. I told you that you should've downsized. You have a lot of stuff to go through."

When I parked, we waited in silence for our parents to arrive. Eiri pulled out her cell phone, and I watched the traffic go by until I saw the moving truck pull into the lot. Poppa pulled the rental truck to the end, far from the other vehicles.

Minnie's was a small, family-run joint that seemed bustling on a weeknight. Upon walking into the quaint entryway, the fragrant aroma of coffee and the clanking of dishes invaded my senses. A few steps inside the door, a hostess was stationed at a wooden podium.

"Welcome! How many in your party?" the hostess asked, her cheery voice loud enough to cut through the diner's noise. I raised my hand to display the number four. It seemed more favorable than yelling over the noise. She grabbed our menus before smiling and saying, "Right this way."

She led us through what felt like half the diner and then gestured to a booth that comfortably sat the four of us. Eiri and I slid into one side while Poppa and Momma occupied the other. The hostess pointed out the two different a la carte menus—one with their specials of the day and the other listing their wide variety of milkshakes.

When we were settled, I reached for the milkshake menu. I couldn't wait to try one of the many flavors they offered. Eiri apparently had the same idea as I did; our hands clashed as we both reached for the menu. We laughed and placed the menu between us so we could both read it.

After a few minutes, our waitress approached the table and greeted us, "Good evening, folks! My name is Betty! I'll be your waitress this evening. Can I get y'all started with something to drink? Coffee? Water? One of our many delicious milkshakes?"

She started with Momma and ended with Poppa, jotting everything down before nodding and asking, "Do y'all need a few more minutes with the menus?" When we all nodded, she told us she'd be back with our drinks in a few minutes and could take our orders then.

Poppa quickly decided what he wanted. Then, he yawned as he ran his large hand down his face, relaxing into the booth. There were bags under his eyes, and he looked exhausted.

"Lily, what are your plans over the next few days? Do you plan to settle in a little bit? Or do you need to get right to work with your experiments?" he asked, his voice tired.

"My experiments don't need to be started yet, thankfully. I need some time to explore the area. You can only learn so much from researching on the internet. I need to see the land for myself; I want to observe the wildlife that inhabits the forest, the level of humidity in the air, and the components of the soil in the gardens. It's an incredible place that I want to become familiar with before jeopardizing my experiments."

He nodded, then let out a short sigh. "Please be careful in those woods. You don't know what lurks out of sight. Promise me that you will be extra cautious of your surroundings while you're out there."

"I'll be fine. I'll make sure to carry my bear mace with me while I walk, and I won't go too far at first," I said, attempting to appease him without making a full promise. To my parents, a promise was an unbreakable oath that someone should never turn their back on. I planned to be vigilant in the woods, but I wasn't sure what was out there yet and didn't want to promise without being sure I wouldn't break it somehow.

Poppa leaned toward me, his eyes darkening with anger. "Anevae, I mean it. Promise me you will be careful."

I leaned back from the table and pressed into the seat. Embarrassment coursed through me, but I still met his gaze. "I'm sorry, Poppa. I promise to be careful."

He pushed himself back with force, stepped out of the booth, and stormed off toward the front of the diner. I lowered my gaze to my hands, tightly clenched in my lap, as a tear rolled down my cheek.

Momma reached across the table in an attempt to calm me. "My Lily, Poppa just wants what's best for you. He also just wants you to be aware of your surroundings. He's right that we don't know what lurks in the woods around your new home," Momma said in a soothing voice as Eiri placed a hand on mine to show her support.

I took an unsteady breath, and my voice cracked as I said, "I know. I don't know what's out there either, and I will be as careful as possible."

We sat there in silence until Betty approached with our drinks. As she sat them down, she said, "Uh-oh. Looks like we're missing a person. Do y'all wanna wait until he gets back?"

We all nodded again, but Momma responded, "Yes, please. Thank you very much. I'm so sorry for making you wait."

"Not a problem! I'll be back in a few," Betty said, flashing a bright smile.

When Poppa returned to the table a short while later, he looked me directly in the eyes and grasped one of my hands that I had replaced on the table. "I'm sorry, Anevae. I'm concerned about leaving you in those woods alone. There can be dangerous creatures just out of sight. I won't be around to protect you any longer. You'll be too far away for me to come to save you in an instant as I've done in the past," he explained just loud enough for me to hear. "You'll always be my little girl, and I'll always be concerned about you no matter what happens. I love you and just want what's best for you."

"I understand, but I'm not a little girl anymore. I have a lot more training and experience now, and I'm *always* cautious when exploring.

"Besides, you can't protect me from everything, no matter how much you want to. I'm a big girl and need to make my own mistakes. I will always call you if something goes wrong and I need your help, but I am capable of taking care of myself," I said, attempting to reassure him.

Betty's timing was impeccable. She returned right at that second to take our orders. Poppa released my hand as Betty collected our orders, retrieved our menus, and headed to the kitchen.

Thankfully, the rest of the dinner was uneventful. After eating, Eiri and I took turns discussing our plans for the next few days until the bill came. As much as I loved my family and knew I'd miss them, I couldn't wait to have a moment to myself again following Poppa's outburst.

I paid the bill, and then we strolled back to the dark, dimly lit parking lot, where we exchanged tearful goodbyes. After several hugs

and well wishes, my family continued toward the moving truck while
I turned in the opposite direction to head back to my SUV. I willed
myself not to cry as I dug my keys out of my jacket pocket to unlock
the car. Once I got in, I took a deep breath and broke down. Poppa
seemed to have a harder time controlling his anger as Eiri and I got
older, but he'd always been protective of us.

# Chapter Three

# Anevae

*A cross the house, I could hear Poppa yelling at Momma in their bedroom. When Poppa came home from work that day, Momma had been telling Eiri and me a story about Caellaias.*

*He was fuming when he heard what she was talking about and wouldn't let it go. Poppa had been scolding Momma for over an hour, and while I couldn't hear everything he was saying to her that day, his main argument was always that Momma shouldn't be telling us these stories.*

*That day, I'd had enough of hearing him yell at her. Momma didn't deserve to be yelled at because she told us stories to entertain us. We asked for them, and it was her way of connecting with us—something Poppa rarely did. He was always busy with work, and when he came home, he frequently disappeared into his office.*

*At the time, I couldn't have been more than ten years old; Eiri was eight and still scared of Poppa when he became irate. As I stomped across the house, she followed, begging me to leave our parents alone. I didn't listen. I was tired of it. I walked up to my parent's bedroom door and pounded on it as hard as I could.*

*I heard shuffling come from inside, and the door flew open. Poppa looked furious at the interruption. "Can't you tell your mother and I are having a conversation, Anevae? Leave us."*

*Puffing out my chest, I stood tall and glared directly into his eyes, yelling, "Momma doesn't deserve to be yelled at like this! She's just trying to entertain us and spend time with us. I sure can't say the same for you!"*

*Poppa reached out and backhanded me. He grabbed my arm before I could hit the floor, pulling me back to my feet. "Lily, you will do what I tell you or suffer the consequences. Leave. Us. Now." Taking a step back, he slammed the door, nearly hitting me in the face, and all I could do was stand in shock.*

*Poppa had never struck me before. I wasn't sure why he had done it then, but tears welled up in my eyes. I refused to let them fall. Turning, I stumbled back to my bedroom, passing a concerned Eiri in the process. When I reached my door, I turned to look at her and just shook my head. I didn't want to talk to her about it, so I just slammed my door closed.*

*As I collapsed onto my bed, I heard heavy footsteps approaching. My door flew open, and Poppa barreled in, gripping my chin tightly. "You brought this upon yourself. If you slam that door again, you will not enjoy your punishment. I expect you to be in the living room in ten minutes minus the damn attitude." He released my chin and stomped out, shutting the door behind him.*

*I took a few deep breaths as tears began to fall down my cheeks. I was stuck between being upset and furious at how Poppa was acting. He'd never treated Eiri or me like that before. I lay there for what felt like an eternity when a soft knock sounded on the door.*

*"Go away!" I shouted, lying back on my bed as I began to sob harder than before. I knew it wasn't Poppa; he would have just barged through the door without knocking again.*

*The door opened, and I looked to see who had come in. When I realized it was Momma, I sat up. Her eyes were bloodshot, and the skin around them was red and puffy—she'd been crying too. I lowered my* head so Momma couldn't look at my face in its entirety. I was sure there was a red mark on my cheek from where Poppa had backhanded me. I wasn't sure she'd seen him hit me, but she may have heard it. Even still, I didn't want her to see the mark it may have left because I knew she'd be upset.

Momma closed the door behind her and came to join me on my bed. As she sat, she grasped my hand and held onto it. "Lily, I'm very sorry you had to see Poppa like that. He doesn't like me talking about Caellaias for a good reason, but sometimes, I can't keep myself from it. One day, you may understand, but today is not that day." Reaching over with her free hand, she caressed my cheek, urging me to look at her.

I winced in pain as she touched the spot where Poppa struck me. She frowned at my reaction and urged me to look at her. As she took in the state of my face, fury flashed in her eyes, and I could swear they began to glow. Then, she was on her feet, rushing out of my room.

"Roarc!" Momma screamed as she yanked the door open and barreled down the hallway. "You will NOT make it a habit to hit our daughters! Need I remind you what I am capable of? If you touch one of them again, I will make you wish you were dead, setting you ablaze from the inside out. You can take your anger out on me all you would like, but I will NOT let you harm them."

I hurried into the hallway behind her and halted in shock at the sight before me. Momma was right in front of Poppa with her finger in his face, scolding him. He was at least seven inches taller and had at least seventy pounds on her, but that didn't stop her.

Running up between my parents, I looked between them. Placing a hand on each of their chests, I tried to shove them apart. "Stop it! You're scaring Eiri!"

Poppa grasped my hand from his chest and wrenched it away before getting in my face again. "Leave. Us. Lily! This is not your battle to fight." When his eyes met mine, his blue irises were rimmed with a vibrant red—something I'd never seen before.

He snarled and shoved me away, then grabbed Momma by the arm and pulled her back toward their bedroom. They yelled back and forth *all along the way, and when they reached their room, he slammed the door shut, cutting us off from their conversation again.*

The painful memory faded, and I wiped away my tears. I took another deep breath and turned on my metalcore playlist to distract me. The music helped soothe my nerves and ease my mind as I drove.

About twenty minutes later, as I drove up the road to my home, I noticed the cabin Eiri had mentioned earlier that day. I couldn't see many details in the dark. The smaller one-story structure appeared to be darker than mine. Lights were on in one of the windows facing the road, which likely meant someone was home. I resolved to set aside time to visit my new neighbor after I got settled. I wanted to introduce myself and hoped they could tell me more about the area. Having someone close to interact with would be great, too.

A small, standing mailbox marked the narrow driveway to my house. I lowered my music so I could concentrate as I turned, keeping alert for any animals lurking.

Once parked, I opened the door and felt the crisp mountain air envelop me. With it being late spring, the temperatures had just started rising, but the night air was still chilly. I looked forward to seeing the snow that would accumulate in the winter, untainted by the dirty streets of a big city. However, I didn't look forward to clearing the snow when it came time to go to town. I wasn't sure how much the area got. Thankfully, I had several months to go before I had to think about it. I just hoped the all-wheel drive on my car would make getting to and from town easier.

I trotted up the steps, opened the front door, and fumbled for the light switch in the dark. Once the light illuminated the room, I kicked my shoes off. I looked around for a place to hang my jacket as I shoved my keys into one of the pockets. When I realized my over-the-door hooks were still packed away, I yanked the jacket off and threw it over the back of the couch. Being a creature of habit, I liked to be able to find things, even if my organization was a little chaotic. It didn't always make sense to everyone else, but it made sense to me, and that was what mattered the most.

It was late, and I'd had a long, exhausting day. Even still, there was so much to do around the house. I sighed and started turning off the lights. I'd done enough for the day.

Once upstairs, I pushed the door to my room open and basked in the soft moonlight pouring in through the window. I found my sheets while we were unloading and set them at the foot of my bed. The clean scent of the black sheets hit my nose as I spread the soft fabric over the mattress. After a few moments of digging through boxes, I found my comforter.

When I finished making my bed, I completed my nightly routine of brushing my teeth, washing my face, and applying moisturizer. My blue eyes stared back at me, bloodshot with deep, dark circles under them. They often changed colors like the varying shades of denim, and on this day, they appeared light and ice-like. My lips were red and chapped from worrying my snakebite piercings and chewing the skin around them, a nervous habit I couldn't seem to break.

I stepped back into my bedroom and grabbed my phone charger and pajamas from my duffel bag. I changed into my night clothes, then opened the window to let in the cool night air. I scrolled through my notifications, searching for anything that needed my immediate attention, but everything there could wait, save for replying to Momma and Eiri's 'goodnight' texts. Finally, I plugged my phone in, turned off the light, and sank into the cool sheets, allowing the crisp mountain air to soothe me to sleep.

# Chapter Four

## *Anevae*

The warm morning sun flooded the room, waking me from a deep sleep. I lay there for a few minutes, allowing myself to wake up a little before dragging myself out of bed and shuffling into the bathroom. I stood at the vanity, brushing my hair and teeth. A good night's sleep had erased some of the redness from my eyes.

My tangled hair was greasy at the roots and desperately needed a wash, but that would have to wait. I had a lot of work that needed to be done, which would just result in me getting dirty again anyway, so there was no point in washing it.

Just after eight, I grabbed my phone from my dresser and headed downstairs. Momma had texted me to let me know she and Poppa had left already, heading back to their place on the East Coast. I replied, telling them to be careful and asking her to let me know when they made it home.

My stomach grumbled as I walked into the kitchen. My parents had insisted on buying me enough groceries to last about a week—enough time to get settled before I had to travel into town for more.

I was delighted to find my coffee maker conveniently placed on the counter near the sink. The box housing my coffee-making supplies was among those scattered across the massive kitchen island. I brewed myself a cup and filled it with lots of creamer and sugar, making it light and sweet—just how I liked it.

Taking a small sip of the hot beverage, I savored its flavor and opened the refrigerator to find something for breakfast. The eggs and sausage I wanted would require pans and cooking utensils. With a sigh, I closed the fridge and set about finding the tools I would need.

I didn't own much in the way of kitchen supplies, so I put them away as I went, setting aside what I needed for breakfast. When I started cooking, the delicious smells permeated the air. My mouth watered, and my stomach grumbled impatiently.

After the last piece of sausage browned nicely, I sat on one of the four bar stools arranged around the island and plotted out my day. Taking my last bite, I cleaned up the mess I made and climbed the stairs to grab my speaker and change clothes. When I moved, I left everything in the drawers to my dresser. While it made the move easier, my clothes got jumbled around. I sifted through the drawers and found some shorts and a tank top to change into so I could be comfortable while I organized.

As I began changing, I saw movement outside my window. Lowering my shirt back down, I rushed to investigate. Just inside the tree line bordering the cabin was a huge, black fox staring at me. Its coat was shiny and laced with streaks of orange throughout. Its bushy tail faded from black and orange to white at the tip. I'd never seen a fox like it; it was captivating.

Standing there staring at it, I realized the fox was watching me too, almost like it was studying me. Then, without warning, it got up and scampered into the woods, quickly drifting out of sight. When I could no longer see it, I reached for my phone to text Eiri. Foxes were her favorite animal. She'd been infatuated with them since we were kids. The first time we saw them at the zoo, she was instantly drawn to their big, bushy tails and the cute sounds they made.

After sending my text, I got changed, grabbed my speaker, and headed downstairs to get started on all the work that needed to be done. I powered on the speaker, put on my favorite metalcore playlist, and set to work.

About an hour later, the boxes littering the island were emptied, and the kitchen was decorated and assembled. Jamming to my music, I felt like I could conquer the whole house by the end of the day.

Filled with motivation, I moved into the living room. I began by moving around the bookshelves into more suitable locations and assigning boxes to each shelf throughout the room. My massive collection of books had to be split between the shelves on either side of the TV stand. Of course, my meticulous personality made sure to rear its ugly head when positioning said books—hardbacks on one shelf, paperbacks on the other. Sets were nestled side-by-side, and books of similar heights were arranged together.

The next box I opened had all of my knick-knacks carefully wrapped and placed in the box so they didn't break in the move. Many of these were sentimental—gifts my mom had given me to remind me of her stories of Caellaias. The first set I unwrapped was a trio of ceramic wolves in different poses. One was standing, another was lying down, and the last was sitting on its haunches, howling. My fingers delicately caressed a crack in one of the back legs of the standing wolf. I had dropped it once, and Momma had had to glue the leg back on. She scolded me about how fragile they were and how I needed to be more careful.

Another set, also made of ceramic, consisted of a beautiful white-winged angel, a black bat-winged demon, and a sweet faerie with wispy, silver wings. She said they were all beautiful and unique in their own way, just like the creatures of Caellaias. A memory of one of Momma's stories flooded my mind.

*"My Flowers! Would you like to hear more about Caellaias this evening?" Momma asked from the end of the hallway.*

*Eiri and I enthusiastically shouted 'Yes!' from our rooms before rushing to the living room and settling on the floor before the couch. Momma took her spot on the couch.*

*Clasping her hands together in her lap, Momma began, "Have I ever told you girls the story about the youngest princess before she ran away?"*

*Eiri and I shook our heads.*

*"A long time ago, a man named Simi took the throne by marrying the princess, Princess Mira, and making her queen. Queen Mira gave birth to two girls ten years apart, Princess Eve and then Princess Laeney. Unfortunately, Queen Mira passed away during the birth of Princess Laeney; the stress was too much for her body. Alone with two children and a kingdom to rule, the king had no choice but to rely heavily on others to care for his girls.*

"Once Laeney was old enough, she began meeting with tutors. They taught her about the kingdom, its history, her magic, how to defend herself, and how to be a perfect lady. As she grew older, one thing that stuck out to her was that her father was obsessed with maintaining a perfect appearance, which was evident in her studies.

"His biggest obsession with maintaining perfection was that every being residing in the castle had to be purebred. Any staff or guards who weren't purebred were excused from their positions upon his coronation. There were always exceptions to the rule, but the King dictated who stayed. He'd also made it clear that the fae weren't to marry outside of their race or species and strongly encouraged this among the other beings in the kingdom as well. He claimed purebred beings were the most powerful and would one day rule all. He himself was a purebred faerie and claimed to be the one true king of Caellaias." Momma's smile faded as she explained the inner workings of the castle.

Her luminous eyes shifted to her hands folded in her lap. A tear fell onto her skirt, and she began sniffling. Eiri and I stared at each other, unsure what to do. I could only think of comforting Momma, so I stood and grabbed Eiri's hand, pulling her with me toward Momma. We embraced her from both sides, attempting to soothe her. She reached around us and pulled us in closely.

When Momma's sniffling ceased, she loosened her grip on us and took a moment to wipe her eyes. "I'm okay, girls. Sit, sit, and I'll finish the story."

Voice hoarse, she continued, "The King expected greatness from Laeney; she was his pride and joy. Her father banned her from attending social events until she came of age so she could focus on her schooling and etiquette training. While this upset her greatly, she did everything she could to make her father proud.

"On her twentieth birthday, her family held a ball at the castle, inviting the lords, ladies, and their families from across the kingdom. The princess was excited to finally interact with the royalty she'd heard so much about. Her father had an ulterior motive for the ball, though. He intended to announce Laeney's engagement to one of the wealthiest *faeries in the realm, even though the faerie was easily as old as her father. When Laeney learned of this, she was petrified. She'd heard awful things about this faerie and did not want to marry him. She pleaded with her father to call off the engagement, but he refused, threatening to lock her up again if she didn't behave like a proper lady," Momma explained.*

*"During the ball, Laeney tried to appear happy; however, she couldn't bring herself to feel anything but disappointment. Her father had kept her hidden, and she had been obedient for many years—now she felt betrayed. She walked around the ballroom and interacted with everyone possible, as she had never had the pleasure of doing so freely before. Little did she know that her father was watching everything she did. None of the interactions mattered to her until she met the Lord of Maiviraea's second son. Instantly, the princess knew he would change her life forever."*

*"What happened to Princess Laeney after, Momma?" I asked.*

*"Did she have to marry the other faerie?" Eiri asked.*

*Momma shook her head. "Maybe another time I'll tell you what happened afterward. You girls need to get ready for bed before Poppa gets home. Run along now."*

# Chapter Five

*Anevae*

I worked until sunset before taking a much-needed shower and retiring to bed. When I woke up the next day, my muscles ached. Two days in a row of moving virtually non-stop was rough on my body, and it needed its rest. After getting out of bed, I threw on some comfy clothes again. My only goal for the day was to organize my bedroom.

Unplugging my phone from the charger, I found a message from Momma letting me know they had arrived home early that morning. I replied to her message, telling her I was glad they made it home safe, I loved them, and to get some much-needed rest after all their work over the last week.

As I walked into the kitchen, the sun shone through the uncovered windows, reflecting off the glossy black granite countertops. All the brand-new appliances were black to match, perfectly complementing the mahogany of the cabin walls and floors.

Once I was done eating, I cleaned up the kitchen and headed back upstairs to work on my bedroom. I filtered through the boxes that littered the room, piece by piece. They were filled to the brim with some of my most prized possessions, ones I would never consider getting rid of. There were too many good memories associated with them. Inside the first box was one of my many jewelry boxes. It contained the majority of the necklaces I had collected over the years, but I hadn't opened the box since I finished high school.

Pulling the doors open, I sifted through the necklaces inside. The first one that caught my eye was the necklace Momma gave me when I turned sixteen. When I pulled it from the jewelry box, the silver chain was cold against my warm hand. I held the delicate pendant close as I admired it. It looked similar to a teal rose, but Momma insisted it was an orletaylaer from Caellaias. Wiping the dust off the dirty pendant, I remembered the day Momma gave it to me.

*I woke up on the day of my sixteenth birthday to snow blanketing the ground. It was a frigid winter day, the perfect weather to curl up on the couch with a warm blanket, some hot cocoa, and a nice book, which I'd do when I was done with breakfast.*

*As I sat up, the delicious aroma of waffles hit me. Momma's waffles were my favorite breakfast food. Excited, I launched myself out of bed and into the bathroom as quickly as possible before running down the hall to the kitchen.*

*Momma greeted me with a bright smile. "Good morning, my Little Lily. Happy birthday! I'm making your favorite for breakfast, but the way you rushed out here, I'm sure you could smell them."*

*"You bet, Momma! I love waffles! You're spoiling me for my birthday." I looked around for my dad and sister, who were nowhere to be seen, so I looked back at Momma, puzzled. "Where are Poppa and Eiri?"*

*Without looking back at me, Momma responded, "Well, Eiri is still asleep. You know she likes her beauty rest. But Poppa got called into work for an urgent matter. He will be back in a little while."*

*"Oh, that's okay. I just hope I get to spend a little bit of time with him today for my birthday," I admitted.*

*I stood there in silence until Momma shooed me off to the table. A few minutes later, she brought me two waffles topped with strawberries and bananas, my two favorite fruits. They smelled amazing, and my mouth watered in anticipation. As soon as she set them down in front of me, I quickly reached for the maple syrup, dumping more than I should have on top. Then, I eagerly dug in and devoured them.*

*Momma giggled as she pulled a small box from her pocket. "I have a special present for you."*

*Setting down my silverware on the plate and pushing it to the side, I turned to give Momma my full attention. I could see the excitement on her face as she handed me the box.*

*"I hope you like it," Momma whispered as I opened the box.*

*Inside was a beautiful silver necklace. The pendant hanging from it looked like a blue rose, but Momma explained, "This is the symbol of our family—an orletaylaer. My mother, your grandmother, gave it to me on my sixteenth birthday, and I wanted to give it to you on yours. And Lily, don't worry about your sister. I have something special for her on her sixteenth birthday as well."*

*I was in awe of the beautiful necklace Momma had given me. She grasped my hand as I went to pull it from the box. Looking up at her, I saw concern in her eyes. "Be careful about Poppa seeing this necklace, please. You know how he feels about Caellaias, and I don't want to upset him, but I wanted you to have a special heirloom from our family."*

*I rose to put the necklace away. If Eiri saw it, she'd likely ask too many questions. If Poppa saw it, he'd be upset and maybe even take the necklace away.*

*As I walked down the hallway, the door to Eiri's room opened, and she rushed toward the kitchen. Knowing she smelled the waffles the same way I had, I laughed under my breath.*

The necklace was beautiful, and I cherished how it reminded me of my family. Since my parents weren't going to be around, I took it out and placed it on my dresser so I could wear it after I was done unpacking. I'd never been able to wear it before.

When I finished going through the jewelry box, I moved on, admiring the beautiful landscape as I went to start on another box. The tall aspens swayed in the light breeze, their leaves putting on a show while the deep green needles of the pines tried to dance in unison, but their stiffness wouldn't quite allow for it. The sky above was a gorgeous light blue with the occasional wispy cloud here and there. I opened the window to let in the delightful scent of the pine trees. Along with it came the trickling of the creek nearby and the rustling of the trees.

The black fox sat, staring at me, a few yards inside the tree line. It was a fascinating creature. Eiri had told me long ago that foxes were inquisitive, but this one seemed more so than I imagined. I knew the creature was curious about the new person that moved to its territory, but it was almost like it was watching me to see what I was doing and how I acted when it came around.

Inching back, I reached for my phone; if it didn't run off first, I wanted a picture for Eiri. I continued to meet its gaze as I sat on the bed and tried to unlock my phone. The moment I took my eyes off the fox, it scurried into the woods.

Saddened that I couldn't get the picture, I went back to my work, opening box after box of my belongings. Along the way, I thought of the good memories that some of my possessions brought up—more gifts from my parents, some of my belongings from my high school years, and even some things from my good college years. A few weren't very pleasant, but I worked hard through them and still graduated with honors.

When the sun began to set outside my window, I glanced at the boxes I had left. Thankfully, I was nearly done, so I stopped for the night, ate, and got ready for bed. As soon as my head hit the pillow, I was out for the night.

# Chapter Six

# *Anevae*

As I woke on my fourth day in the new home, the stiffness in my muscles screamed at me to take it easy. After my bedroom, the only project left was the greenhouse, and it could wait for the time being.

The monotonous unpacking process had me feeling stir-crazy, which I thoroughly despised. When I was finished with my bedroom, I contemplated exploring my property because it would be helpful to know the land before I started my first experiments outside. But I wasn't worried about starting experiments for several more days and wanted to relax if possible.

As an introvert, being in contact with my family was usually enough to keep my social needs met—it was even draining at times. But the urge to socialize was nagging at me. My mind kept wandering to the neighbor in the small cabin nearby. If anyone were living there, they would have better knowledge of the area and wildlife, so it made sense for me to wander over for a visit.

After breakfast, I jumped in the shower. Then, I wrapped a fluffy towel around me in search of some clothes. I needed something that looked presentable but was easy to move around in, so I pulled a pair of jeans and a T-shirt out of the closet. When I was done, I put a little makeup on before heading downstairs to grab my keys and head toward the neighbor's house.

The other cabin was only about two miles away, but I didn't know anything about the woods yet, so I drove the short distance. Nervousness coiled inside of me during my drive; I was always anxious about meeting new people. Was this someone who didn't want any visitors? Would they send me away rather than invite me in? Or would they be friendly and welcoming?

Pulling into the neighbor's driveway, I joined a black, dirt-covered SUV at the back of the cabin. It looked as if it hadn't been used for a while. Doubt consumed me. Was I wrong about the light being on the other night? Did this neighbor have multiple cars and just not use this one often?

*Stop being so anxious and just go knock on the door,* I scolded myself. There was no point in speculating. After a few deep breaths, I proceeded to the front door. Knocking loudly, I took a step back and waited for a response. With no answer after a couple of minutes, I knocked again. When there was no answer on the second attempt either, I turned to leave.

I was a few steps away when the door swung open behind me. Spinning on the spot, I found a tall, beautiful woman standing in the doorway. While I stood at five foot five, the woman before me had to be at least four inches taller, with smooth, olive-toned skin. Her pear-shaped body showed off her luscious curves and long legs. She had long, curly, jet-black hair with orange streaks throughout and doe-eyes the color of a bright orange sunrise. Her adorable snub nose was positioned perfectly above her pink, bow-shaped lips. Those heavenly lips instantly beckoned for me to kiss them.

Thankfully, I had some semblance of self-control as I gazed back into her mesmerizing eyes and stuttered, "H-hi there."

One of her thick, black brows raised in confusion. "Hello? Can I help you?" she asked as she peered around me.

I quickly cleared my throat before saying, "My name is Anevae. I just moved into the cabin up the way and wanted to stop by to introduce myself."

She chuckled and offered her slim, dainty hand. "My name is Maeyve. It's nice to meet you, Anevae. Such a beautiful name."

Hearing her honeyed voice say my name sent shivers down my spine. I wanted to get lost in the sound.

Grasping her hand, I felt a tingling sensation travel up my arm. Shocked by the sensation, I tried not to let it show as I shook her hand. "It's very nice to make your acquaintance, Maeyve. And thank you."

Scrunching her nose, she giggled. "You aren't from around here, are you?"

Shaking my head, I stammered, "Well, no, I'm not. I'm actually from the East Coast, but that doesn't explain my formality. I blame that on my mom. She's spoken formally all my life, and it's rubbed off a little."

She smiled brightly as I spoke, flashing her pearly white teeth. "That's sweet. What brings you to the area?"

Clasping my hands together, I fiddled with my thumbs, willing myself to refocus on the conversation. "I moved out here for my work. It's a beautiful place, and I'm excited to explore it. If I may ask, how long have you lived here?"

Maeyve's smile waned as she bit the inside of her cheek. "Well, um, I've been here for quite some time. I'm not really sure exactly how long anymore. The years have blurred together."

"Oh." My brow furrowed. She couldn't have been more than twenty-nine. Unless she inherited this home from a parent, I couldn't imagine she'd lived in the cabin long enough to have forgotten when she moved in. "If it's not too much of a bother, I would love to hear more about the area from someone with firsthand experience. I did some research before moving out here; however, that has only gone so far. Anything you can tell me about what I might run into in these woods would be helpful."

Maeyve's smile returned. "If that's the case, we could be here for a while. There's a lot to tell. Would you like to come inside?"

It took me a moment to answer as I didn't know the woman, but I couldn't deny the pull I felt toward her. A feeling in my gut told me that she'd never hurt me. "That would be great, actually," I responded with a smile.

Maeyve took a step back to open the door wider. Hesitantly, I took a step inside. As I crossed the threshold, warmth engulfed me. The intense aroma of vanilla and berries closely followed. After the initial shock, I moved aside so Maeyve could close the door, kicking my shoes off by the door. She led me down a short hallway that opened up into a large room with a high ceiling. I came to an abrupt stop. From the outside, you would never expect a room this size. The decorations Maeyve chose accentuated the dark ebony wood of the walls perfectly.

Returning my gaze to Maeyve, the light caught one of the orange streaks in her hair. The color matched her strange but mesmerizing eyes. Surely, it was dyed, but it was beautiful either way.

"Please have a seat," she said, motioning toward the large sectional in the middle of the room. "Can I get you anything? Water? Tea? Coffee?"

I nodded and quietly responded, "I'd love some water, please. I appreciate you inviting me inside."

Maeyve smiled widely again. "Of course! I love having visitors. Unfortunately, I don't get many out here." Then, she turned toward the kitchen.

I stood there, admiring the space, until I heard Maeyve return. Turning my attention back to her, she handed me the water I requested. I sat cross-legged at one end of the couch, and she did the same at the other end, putting some space between us. I chuckled at the similarities in our posture.

"Your cabin is breathtaking," I said as I looked around again. Holding her gaze set loose a million butterflies in my belly. She was gorgeous, and I never wanted to look away from her enticing doe-eyes, but I also didn't want to make a fool of myself.

Maeyve chuckled and sat back. "Thank you. It's been a work in progress for a long time."

I quirked my head and worried my lip ring, trying to place just how old she was. How many years could she have really lived here on her own?

She folded her hands in her lap as our eyes met again. "I've tried hard to make this cabin feel like home for so long. My family abandoned me many years ago. I don't go into town often, either."

"I'm sorry to hear about your family. I couldn't imagine. What about the previous tenants of my cabin? Did you ever talk to them?"

"I'm sorry. I didn't mean to just dump all of that on you," she said, lowering her gaze to her hands as her cheeks reddened. "There hasn't been anyone in your cabin for several years, and before that, I rarely saw anyone there. I think it was someone's secondary vacation home."

"Interesting. It's in pristine condition. It doesn't seem like it's been vacant at all. Why don't you go into town?"

"Well, um, I'm not really a people person. Big crowds make me nervous and uncomfortable." She took a deep breath and looked back up at me. "That's enough about me for now. Let's get to the real reason you came here. What would you like to know about the area? Exploring the woods is one of my favorite things to do. I've visited every inch of them."

"Honestly, I'd love to hear anything you're willing to share."

"I'd love to tell you all I know, but I have a feeling you'd appreciate it even more if you could experience it. Maybe, once you're feeling settled and rested enough, we can venture out together, and I can introduce you to the area."

"That would be amazing!"

"Perfect! Why did you choose this area to move to?"

"Well, I'm a biological engineer who focuses mainly on agriculture. The cabin was perfect for my needs; with several garden plots outside and a massive greenhouse attached to it, I'll have plenty of space to run my experiments. I was hired by a Colorado-based company—Vision for the Future—to run experiments using a special additive that hasn't yet been released to the public."

"That's interesting. What kind of additive is it?" she asked, head tilted to the side.

"Well, it's a liquid full of nutrients you can add to soil. Soil typically needs several different nutrients—potassium, nitrogen, phosphorus, and manganese, to name a few—to grow plants well. Several of the liquid additives on the market boast their use of the first three, but my company wants to see how well plants grow with higher levels of manganese, too."

"So the nutrients in the additive are already in the soil, just not in the concentrations you're using, right?"

"Correct. I'll be using the additive in controlled environments—the garden plots and pots inside my greenhouse. It shouldn't harm the existing plants or soil, but I don't know for sure yet, so I'm trying to err on the side of caution. I'd also like to keep the animals in the area away from it, just in case."

"That sounds like a great idea. Most of the animals stay away from humans around here, but you can never be too careful."

"Absolutely. What kinds of animals are there around here?"

"We have a lot of rabbits, deer, and foxes running around. There are also some bears and wolves around, too. So just be careful about going out too far."

My heart rate spiked at the thought of running into a bear. They're massive creatures and could easily rip a person to shreds. I shivered at the thought.

"Are there any plants I should be wary of?" I asked.

"Not really. The usual poison ivy, stinging nettle, and poison oak are around, but they're not super common."

"I'll keep an eye out for those. Thank you!"

We sat there for a moment in silence, sipping our drinks. Then she asked, "Where are you moving here from?"

"I've spent my whole life in Connecticut. Most recently, I was living just outside the capital—Hartford. It was beautiful, but way too busy for me. I hate the hustle and bustle of city living; I needed the peace and quiet of the outdoors. That's another reason I chose the cabin."

"That makes sense. I also grew up in a busy area, so I get it."

"Oh. So you didn't grow up around here?" I asked, raising an eyebrow.

She stilled, and her eyes grew wide. "Um, no. I didn't, but when I was able to get away, this was my escape. I've always loved it here."

"Well, I'm glad you were able to find your escape. Do you mind sharing it? Because this may very well be my escape, too."

She huffed out a laugh as she rolled her bottom lip into her mouth. When she released it, she said, "I don't think I'd mind sharing it with you."

I took another sip of my water and looked out the window, trying to hide my flushed cheeks. Thunder rumbled in the distance, and splotches of rain dotted the glass. The sky was dark and cloudy. *Had the sun already set? How long had we been talking?*

"Wow. It doesn't feel like we've been here for long, but it's already dark out. I should get out of your hair, and I'm getting tired." I turned my attention back to her and gave a small smile. "I appreciate your hospitality. It's been great to sit here and talk to you."

"Do you have plans tomorrow?" Maeyve asked.

"I haven't thought that far ahead yet. I'm completely unpacked, save for the greenhouse, and I'd love to see the area before I get it set up. I want to see what I can manage outside versus inside."

"Would you like to go on a little adventure tomorrow? I can show you around a little bit," she said, a hopeful look in her eyes.

"I'd love that, but I don't want to interfere with anything you've got going on."

The corner of her mouth tipped up in a half-smile. "I don't have anything going on. That's why I asked."

"Oh! In that case, I'd love to!" I said, heart racing with excitement.

Her smile grew, and her eyes lit up. "Great! Why don't you come over at about eight tomorrow morning? Make sure to pack lots of snacks and water. We'll probably be out all day."

"Sounds like a plan! I look forward to it."

"I've enjoyed your company and look forward to spending more time with you."

Setting down my glass, I climbed off the couch and stretched again. She did the same. *How long had we been sitting there?*

After we exchanged goodbyes, she walked me to the door, where I stepped out into the rain and hurried to my car. When I pulled back up to my cabin, I was exhausted mentally and physically. Yet I felt more alive inside than I had at any other time in my life, especially around another person.

Once inside, I shed my wet coat, ate a quick dinner, and headed to my room to finish my nightly routine. While brushing my teeth, I caught sight of myself and took a double-take. My eyes were more vibrant and lively than usual, and I couldn't shake the smile that was now permanently plastered to my face.

When I was done, I changed into my pajamas and set my alarms, not wanting to miss my meeting with Maeyve. Without them, I couldn't trust myself to wake up on time. After crawling into bed, I listened to the steady pitter-pattering of the rain on the windows, lulling me to sleep.

# Chapter Seven

## Maeyve

When Anevae left, I sat back on the couch, stunned by the incredible woman who seemed to magically appear at my door as if I'd summoned her. I knew the moment she came into my territory. I'd already scoped her out several times since she moved in because, true to the nature of a fox, I was curious about the world. But I never expected her to come to me.

After our introductions, we shook hands, and that's when I felt an unfamiliar zap travel up my arm. I'd never felt anything like it and knew I needed to learn more about her. A wave of relief washed over me when I was able to invite her in; she wanted to know more about the area, and I was happy to oblige. As soon as she walked in, her scent hit me. She was a being of Caellaias. When she walked in, I tried to determine what kind, but her scent was too muted.

I wandered to the back door with my mind still trying to process what had just happened. I felt the need to make sure she had gotten home okay, and I was still downright intrigued by her. The rain had let up since she left, so I wouldn't be as soaked as if I'd gone out immediately after. As much as I loved the feeling of my fur being wet, I didn't like being drenched.

Stripping off my clothes, I walked out onto the porch and took a deep breath. When I stepped into the rain, it was frigid on my warm skin, but it felt good at the same time. Ever since I'd shaken Anevae's hand, I felt like I was on fire.

Kneeling on the grass, I took a few deep breaths. As I inhaled the smell of the rain and wet grass, I placed my hands on the ground and began shifting. My bones broke and repositioned themselves to conform to the shape of my fox form. My fur began to grow, my face reshaped itself, and my hands began to shift into paws. The pain from shifting was nowhere near as painful as it had been the very first time. I'd grown more accustomed to my second skin the more I shifted.

After my shift was complete, I used my enhanced eyesight to take in my surroundings, looking for any wildlife. It was also possible another creature from Caellaias was around. Every few years, I'd run into a lost being and have to help them find their way back into the kingdom or into the human realm because they didn't want to return to Caellaias for one reason or another. There wasn't any movement nearby that I could see, so I turned to my other senses.

Lifting my nose, I attempted to identify any unusual scents around me. The rain masked most scents, but it was always worth a shot. If a smell was strong enough, I'd still be able to detect it.

Closing my eyes, I focused on the sounds of the forest. There was the light pitter-patter of rain, the leaves rustling from the light breeze blowing through the area, and the trickling of the nearby creek. There wasn't anything unusual.

With my assessment of the area complete, I trotted through the forest toward Anevae's cabin. I was caught off-guard the first time I tried to go onto her property. One of the strongest protection wards I'd ever encountered had been placed on the land. The presence of it made me suspicious; it hadn't been there before she moved in. A fae created the ward, and another powerful being sealed it, but their scents were covered to conceal their identities. The beings were good—I'd give them that—but what were they protecting this woman from?

During her time with me that day, she showed no signs of knowing that a portal to Caellaias was nearby. I'd seen how oblivious she seemed to the dangers the woods could possess over the last few days, so I wondered if she had any knowledge of the kingdom at all. Did she even know she was a being of Caellaias? She didn't act like it. And she told me she'd grown up in a big city. Was that true, or was she hiding something?

Thanks to the ward, I couldn't cross onto her property without her permission, so I was stuck at the tree line. I'd sat there several times since she'd moved in, just watching her. I was glad the ward was there to protect her when I couldn't because I felt this innate need to do so. I didn't understand it yet, but I hoped to learn more as I spent time with her. She was interesting and different from anyone I'd ever met; I wanted to figure her out. While I watched her, I let my curiosity get the best of me all too often. I wasn't doing a great job keeping myself hidden from her—she'd seen me more than once already and even tried to take pictures of me.

When I approached my boundary, the light in the kitchen turned off. Her curvy frame was illuminated in the bedroom window a few moments later. She was beautiful, unlike any woman I'd ever met before. She had these striking blue eyes and plump, naturally red lips that starkly contrasted her pale skin. Her crimson-red hair was a mass of voluminous waves that looked perfect no matter how she styled it. Her button nose and high cheekbones were covered in tiny freckles, making her eyes even more vibrant. Every time I trailed my eyes down her body, her curves and thick thighs made my mouth water. I'd always liked a woman with some extra meat on her bones, but I hadn't looked at a woman—anyone really—that way in years. I'd been through too much during my time in Caellaias to consider being with anyone intimately.

I watched Anevae walk in and out of the bathroom, getting ready for bed. When she approached her dresser, she pulled out a pair of pajamas and began stripping. My pulse quickened as she took off her shorts, revealing a pair of bright red lace panties. A pulsing started in my clit, and I looked away. As much as I wanted to sit there and see her beautiful body, I didn't want her to realize I was there watching her get undressed.

On the way back to my cabin, I decided to go for a hunt. I still had enough food to last me for a few months, but I hadn't heard from Arturo in several weeks. He was a bear shifter I'd met many years prior who'd been helping me with food and other supplies in exchange for help with odd jobs at his general store in Fawnhaven. We weren't what you'd consider friends, more like business partners, so we didn't keep in constant contact.

I did try to reach out to him a few times before Anevae's arrival to the area with no response and I hadn't made it into town to see if everything was okay. I avoided human contact as much as possible since I didn't age like them. I still appeared in my mid to late twenties and had looked that way for many years. Anevae was also a huge distraction, and I didn't want to let her out of my sight.

With the rain that night, it took me longer than average to locate my prey—a rabbit. I carried it home and placed it on the porch so I could shift back to my human form. When I had fully functioning hands again, I used the spigot outside to clean some of the mud off myself. After the last large clump of dirt was rinsed from my skin, I turned off the spigot and grabbed the rabbit, heading inside.

Stepping over the threshold, I grabbed a towel off the shelf. I had left them there for days when I was wet or dirty after a shift. I tried to clean off the smears of mud left on my arms and legs, but a shower was going to be necessary to get it out of my hair. When I was done wiping myself off, I dropped the towel on the floor with my dirty clothes and then turned to the kitchen.

I found my favorite knife and got to work dressing the rabbit. It was a messy process, so I was glad I had waited to take a shower. After it was dressed, I grabbed a pan and got to work making my dinner.

When I was done eating, I cleaned up the kitchen and made my way to the bathroom, grabbing my dirty laundry on the way. After dropping everything in the hamper, I turned on the water until it was almost too hot to handle and stepped into the stream. The harsh contrast between the hot water and my cool skin caused me to jump, but I relaxed under the warmth once my body got used to the temperature. As I cleaned my body, all I could think about was how it would feel to have Anevae's body against mine. I thought about how it would feel to have her hands skimming over my skin the way the water was.

A strong pulsing started in my clit again. I couldn't let the thought of her consume me—at least not yet. I also didn't want the darker parts of me to ruin her. I hardly knew anything about her besides what I'd seen and what she'd told me that day. I couldn't shake the feelings of how she made me feel and my attraction to her.

I forced myself to get out of the shower and push the beautiful woman from my mind, grabbing the clean towel from the rack as I stepped out. After drying off, I went back to my bedroom to grab some pajamas. I wanted to get up early the next morning; Anevae was coming to explore the area with me. I needed to make a plan of where we'd be going and what I needed to pack. The thought that I'd be near her again had my heart racing in excitement. I slid the soft fabric of my pajamas over my skin and climbed into bed. As I laid my head down, I drifted off to visions of the strange but gorgeous woman filling my head.

# Chapter Eight

# *Anevae*

I woke feeling refreshed and excited for the day. The thought of seeing Maeyve again invigorated me. Once I got out of bed, I dressed and gathered supplies for our adventure.

After making some coffee and a small breakfast with my diminishing food supply, I sat down to eat. The thought of needing groceries reminded me that I hadn't checked in with my sister in a couple of days. Pulling out my phone, I texted her.

*How's it going? Still unpacking?*

I'm only like halfway through! I hate to say it, but maybe I should have listened to you… This is ridiculous!

How's your stuff coming along? My luck, you're probably already done and ready to gloat.

I would NEVER gloat about the fact that I finished early yesterday because I was smart and downsized a bunch.

You're such a liar and so RUDE! Why do you have to be like that?!

If you're already done, maybe you could help me?! Please?

How the hell did you get done so fast anyway?!

I'm done because I DOWNSIZED. You really should have listened.

And I would help you, but I have plans. I went down to the neighbor's house yesterday, and she's showing me around today…

You're doing WHAT?! Are you stupid?! This person could be a serial killer or something!

What the hell are y'all going to do? Frolic through the meadows and pick daisies?

Would you listen to yourself?!

She's extremely nice, and we talked for hours. She said she's seen every inch of this forest and offered to show me around.

So you ARE going to frolic through the meadows and pick daisies.

Are you nuts? You don't even know her!

Did you go into her home?!

I'm glad you're telling me where you're going and who you're going with so we'll know who to blame when you go missing.

I love you and appreciate your concern, but we are grown women. Let me make my mistakes, just as you've made yours.

I can take care of myself, and I'm not going into all this unprepared. I'm bringing my bear mace and a pocket knife. Nothing is going to happen to me.

When I met this woman, there was an immediate connection. I wouldn't have gone into her home if I hadn't felt comfortable. There's something about her I can't explain.

Again, I love you, and I'll let you know when I get home.

With a heavy sigh, I shoved my phone into my pocket and finished my remaining breakfast. Eiri wasn't wrong, but she wasn't there when everything happened; I knew deep down I could trust Maeyve. Even thinking about the gorgeous woman, butterflies were erupting in the pit of my stomach.

After breakfast, I had about ten minutes until I was supposed to meet Maeyve at her cabin. Being late was one of my biggest pet peeves, and it made me anxious. I rushed to put my boots on and find my jacket, keys, and backpack.

As I wrapped up, I burst through the door, rushing to my SUV. Pressing the button to unlock the vehicle, I reached for the handle when I realized I had forgotten to lock the front door. Frustrated with myself, I stomped back up the steps. I didn't need to worry about it being this far away from town, but it made me feel more comfortable. When I was absolutely sure I had locked the door, I returned to my SUV and hurried off.

Turning onto her driveway, I glanced at the clock again. 8 a.m. on the dot! After I parked, I grabbed my backpack and approached the front door. As I raised my hand to knock, the door swung open, revealing a smiling Maeyve dressed in all black. Her clothes were tight, accentuating her pear-shaped physique, making it hard for me not to stare at her again.

Straightening myself out, I greeted her with a cheery smile, "Good morning!"

She smiled brightly. "Good morning. Please come in while I finish packing my bag."

I sat on the couch, waiting patiently. When she was done rounding her things up, she dropped her backpack by the front door and grabbed her boots to sit next to me so she could lace them up.

As she finished, she grinned at me. "Are you ready?"

When I nodded, she smiled and grasped my hand. As soon as our hands connected, that same tingling sensation surged through my body again. If she felt it, she didn't react. She pulled me off the couch toward the front door, grabbing her backpack so we could head out.

Maeyve locked up and then walked up beside me as I peered into the tree line. "What are you looking at? Or are you looking for something?" she asked, studying the tree line alongside me.

"I was just waiting for you." Turning to her, I asked, "Did I tell you I saw a fox the other day? It was black with some orange and a tail that was tipped white. I've never seen one like it before." She met my gaze, concerned etched in her features. *Why would she be worried about that?*

The look was gone as soon as it had come. "That's interesting. I've seen foxes in the area, but never one like you described. Anyway, there's a lot of stuff I want to show you, and we don't want to be stuck in the woods with only moonlight leading the way. Are you ready?"

"Absolutely!"

"Perfect! Well, let's introduce you to my neck of the woods!" Grasping my hand again, she dragged me out to the tree line.

The first place we stopped was an aquamarine-colored, milky lake near her cabin. Creatures beneath the surface were causing bubbles to break the surface tension, and a large fish jumped, creating ripples across the water.

A little further along, we came across a large meadow filled with flowers just beginning to bloom. It was my favorite spot throughout the whole adventure, and it smelled amazing.

We found a spot in the meadow, clear of flowers, so we could eat lunch and relax for a while. I was pleasantly surprised when Maeyve pulled a blanket out of her pack for us to sit on—the ground was still damp from the rain the night before. Thankfully, the sun was high in the sky, and there wasn't any sign of clouds that would threaten our time together.

When we finished up our lunches, we continued our expedition. True to what she'd told me, we saw rabbits, birds, squirrels, deer, and foxes.

As the day wound down, we headed back to Maeyve's. The sun had just disappeared behind the trees when we reached her cabin. I stood there awkwardly, watching the colors of the sky change. I knew I should get going home.

"I should –" I began to say.

"Would you –" she said at the same time.

"Oops. Go ahead," I said, looking back at her and encouraging her to go first with a smile.

She let out a nervous laugh. "I was going to ask if you'd like to keep me company for a little longer. I was thinking about making some beef stroganoff if you're interested?" When she was done speaking, she bit her lip and had a hopeful look in her eyes.

My eyes grew wide, and I swore my heart stopped. "I, uh, feel like I've already taken up so much of your time today. I should –"

"Nonsense! I've enjoyed spending time with you. Seriously. Please?" she asked, holding her hand out to me with big puppy dog eyes and a pouty lip.

I grabbed her hand with a smile. "I'd love to."

She led me into the house, and I settled onto the couch while she got to work. I hadn't noticed the day prior, but there was a half-wall that allowed you to look directly into the kitchen so I could talk to her from where I was.

When the scents of the food hit me, I let out a low groan. "That smells delicious."

Maeyve looked up at me with a smile on her face. "Thank you! It's one of my favorites. Speaking of, what's your favorite food?"

"Lasagna, but I love anything with noodles or potatoes, really."

After my response, she turned her attention back to the food. "Interesting! What's your favorite drink?"

I let out a small laugh and raised one of my eyebrows as I asked, "Are we talking alcoholic or non-alcoholic?"

"Hmm. How about both?"

"Ooh. Let's see. If I had to pick something non-alcoholic, I'd probably say Diet Dr. Pepper or cream soda. As far as alcoholic drinks, I'm stuck between a good margarita and a Malibu sunset. Both are really good, but I'm a rum girly. What about you?"

"I love apple juice, and I'm not really a big drinker, but I'm always down for a good margarita," she said with a smirk.

"Hmm. That's interesting. Okay. How about your favorite movie?"

She stopped stirring the food and glanced back up at me. "I haven't really watched a movie in a long time."

My mouth dropped open, and my eyes grew to the size of saucers. "Seriously? Oh, man. I know *exactly* what we're doing one of these days! I have a huge movie collection. You've gotta see my favorite – 'The Queen of the Damned.' Ooh! And 'Inside Out!' I know, I know. 'Inside Out' is a kid's movie, but it's *sooooooo* good!"

She let out another nervous laugh and went back to stirring the food. "That would be fun." Then, she glanced back at me through her eyelashes. "Does that mean you want to spend more time with me?"

My heart stuttered as I took in the way she was looking at me. Biting my lip piercing, I nodded. When I released it, I whispered, "I'd love to spend more time with you."

A smile spread across her face, and she returned her focus to the food again. I stared at her for several moments, wondering what was going through her head.

When dinner was done, she served us each a plate. We sat opposite each other on the couch in identical positions again.

After blowing on the piping hot food, I took a small bite. The flavors exploded in my mouth as soon as it hit my tongue. My hand covered my mouth as I chewed the food.

Looking at Maeyve, I said, "Oh my god. This tastes amazing! I've had beef stroganoff before, but this is the best one I've ever tasted!"

"I'm glad you like it," she said with a smile before taking a bite of her own.

"I don't just like it; I love it! I've eaten so much fast food over the last few weeks. This is a nice change. Most of my meals at home have been quick and easy since I don't have much in the way of groceries. My parents brought me enough to get through my first week. I'll probably head down to Havenridge the day after tomorrow. My sister just moved into an apartment down there."

She tilted her head to the side as she finished chewing. After swallowing her food, she asked, "How many siblings do you have?"

Between bites, I answered her, "I just have the one. We're two years apart, and we tell each other basically everything. She wanted to come with me when I told her I was moving out here. She prefers city living, though, so she got the apartment in Havenridge."

"What's her name? If you don't mind me asking."

"It's Eirian, but we call her Eiri for short."

"That's a really pretty name. I've never heard it before."

"Our parents didn't want something common for either of us. I'm not sure where they got our names from."

"Well, they're both beautiful."

I blushed as I met her gaze. "Thank you. I've never met someone named Maeyve, but I've heard the name several times. It fits you."

"Thank you."

"You're welcome. Do you have any siblings?"

"No, I don't think I do. My dad took off before I was born, so I know nothing about him. My mom never had any other children."

"I'm so sorry about your dad."

"It's okay. From what I've heard, he wasn't a great guy. Anyway, tell me about your parents."

"Well, I've always been pretty close to my parents. My mom was a stay-at-home mom, but my dad was a workaholic. Throughout my life, they've always supported me in my endeavors. When I told them I'd be moving out here for work, they were concerned. They tried to convince me not to move out here at all."

"Why?"

"My parents have always been very protective of me. I went through a really rough spot while I was in college, and they had to help me put the pieces of my life back together. Thankfully, I wasn't far from home at the time. Moving out here, I'm over a day's drive away, so they can't save me if something bad happens."

"I'm sorry."

"It's okay. It's in the past, and I'm not the same person as I was back then. I've done a lot to make myself more comfortable and confident; I don't need my parents to save me from everything anymore."

"That's good to hear. It's a great way to look at things."

"It is." I looked down at my empty plate and then back up at her. "I should get home. I appreciate everything today."

After taking the last bite of her food, she reached to grab my plate. "Let me go put these away. I'll be right back."

When she returned, she sat on the edge of the couch. "Would you, um, like to come over again tomorrow? There's another place I'd like to take you."

"I'd love that! I'm enjoying spending time with you."

"I really enjoy spending time with you, too."

"Should I meet you here at the same time as today?"

"Sounds perfect." Smiling, she rose from the couch and offered me her hand. Taking it, she helped me off the couch and walked me to the door.

After putting on my shoes, I wrapped her in a quick hug and said, "Have a good night. I'll see you in the morning."

"I'll see you in the morning."

The entire drive home, my stomach was full of butterflies. Being around her, talking to her, it all felt so natural. She made me feel comfortable like no one else had before. The day had been perfect, and I found myself giddy about seeing her again.

When I got home, I went into the kitchen to grab some water. Walking past the sink, I glanced out the window. The floodlights were on, and the black fox sat just inside the tree line again, staring intently at me. When I reached for my phone, it scurried into the darkness.

After a few minutes of hoping the fox would return, I gave up and went upstairs to get ready for bed. Despite my exhaustion from the adventure with Maeyve, my mind was stuck on the beautiful creature. I was amazed to hear that Maeyve hadn't seen it, especially because she'd been in the area for so long. The fox wasn't a pup and seemed comfortable in the area, which led me to believe it had been around for a while.

Before heading to bed, I took a quick shower and then texted my sister to tell her I was okay and had made it home safely. With my eyes heavy, I crawled into bed and quickly drifted into a deep sleep.

# Chapter Nine

## Maeyve

After I walked Anevae to the front door, I rushed to the back door, ripping my clothes off piece by piece as I went. Throwing the door open, I shifted and took off. I had to make sure she got home; the need to protect her was overwhelming.

When I approached her property, I got as close as I could without getting hurt or forced back. I wasn't willing to find out what would happen if I crossed the threshold without permission. The power behind the ward was so intense I was worried it could kill me.

Anevae's SUV pulled up on the other side of the cabin as I waited. Foxes are able to run about thirty miles an hour, and with the added advantage of cutting through the woods, I made it well before her.

The light turned on in the kitchen, and I spotted her crimson-red hair through the window. On her way to the fridge, she glanced out the window and paused. *Shit, I triggered the floodlight.* She stared at me with those breathtaking blue eyes. Her beautiful, plump lips slightly parted with awe. I knew my fox was beautiful; numerous people had told me, but I wanted her to look at me—in either form—the way she was then for the rest of my days.

We stared at each other until she shifted her stance, reaching into her pocket. She was likely trying to take a photo again. I couldn't let that happen because I knew she'd have too many questions, so I turned tail and ran.

I panicked when she brought up my fox form earlier in the day. I didn't want to lie to her, but I couldn't let her know about me yet. Call me selfish, but I wanted her to think I was just another creature in the woods until I could figure her out. I needed to start being more careful about how much she saw me.

I ran for about a mile before I stopped. I knew I'd be out of her line of sight, so I waited several minutes before returning to her property line. I couldn't help myself. She was like an invisible force that kept pulling me back to her. She was supposed to visit again in the morning, but that wasn't enough.

While I sat there, I spotted her in her bedroom window again. I'd caught her when she was fully undressed and getting ready for bed. Her pale skin glowed in the moonlight, illuminating all of her perfect features. Her voluptuous hourglass figure was facing the window, displaying her large breasts, beautiful belly, wide hips, and thick thighs. The stretch marks that spread across her stomach and large breasts were a light pink. One day, I'd love to kiss all over her body and show her how beautiful she really was.

Keeping my hands off her was becoming increasingly more challenging as I spent more time with her—and when I caught her in these intimate moments. I scurried into the woods before it became too overwhelming to resist. It had been so long since I'd fed the other part of me. I had to go home and attend to it before I could no longer resist the urge.

Once again, I was covered in mud, so I went to the lake near my home and cleaned myself up. The milky water was cool against my all-too-hot skin, making me feel a little more comfortable.

After swimming for a while, I climbed back onto the shore and returned to my human form. Sitting there, I tried to compose myself, but I was fighting a battle I wouldn't win. Knowing it was pointless to keep fighting it, I gave up and returned to my cabin. Even though it was a short trip, it felt like an eternity. I wanted nothing more than to return to Anevae's, but I knew it would do me no good because I couldn't even get onto her property.

Once at my back door, I wiped my feet on the rug before stepping inside, grabbing a towel, and shutting the door behind me. I wiped off any residual mud and sand I could, but I was still covered, so I headed straight for the shower.

After starting the water, I deposited my towel in the hamper and glanced at myself in the mirror. Catching a glimpse of my eyes, I had to do a double take. They were the brightest orange I'd ever seen.

My mind and body reacted so strangely to the mere thought of Anevae. It was like I was burning up from the inside out and constantly wanted to be near her. When I did touch her, it felt like I would explode. I'd never learned about this kind of reaction, nor had I ever felt it before. I had gone years without being touched by another, and my body didn't care; my other half didn't care either. But from the first moment I saw Anevae, I became obsessed with her. Being so close and unable to touch her how I wanted was frustrating.

As I climbed into the shower, the hot water hit my skin, only adding fuel to the fire within. I leaned against the shower wall and let the water caress my body. I imagined Anevae was with me, and the water was her hands grazing across every inch of my skin. A pulsing ramped up in my center, one I couldn't ignore any longer. Gliding my hand over my body, I slid it between my thighs.

Lightly grazing over my clit, I let out a soft moan. It had been so long since I'd touched myself, and I was already sensitive. I slowly rubbed circles on the sensitive area as the pulsing increased in intensity. With my other hand, I reached for my breast and pinched my nipple. Gasping, I could already feel my climax rising. I knew I wouldn't last long, and moments later, I was coming.

For the first time in years, I felt alive on the inside again.

61

# Chapter Ten

# Maeyve

The following day, I rolled out of bed at 7 a.m. It was the best I had slept in years, but when I realized the time, I started rushing around the house to get things cleaned up. Anevae was supposed to be at my cabin in one hour, but my clothes were still strewn across the house from my quick shift, and I hadn't taken care of the dishes from dinner the night prior.

When I was done cleaning up, I had about ten minutes before she was set to arrive. I threw together a quick breakfast and then started replenishing the supplies in my backpack. I was about halfway done when I heard Anevae's car pull up. I left everything sprawled across the bed and sprinted to the door to greet her.

On the way there, I caught a glimpse of myself in the mirror in the hallway. My appearance was disheveled, but I couldn't help staring. In the mirror was a version of myself I had never seen before. My orange eyes were vibrant and full of life, my cheeks rosy, and I had a smile on my face. For the first time in years, I didn't look miserable; I looked...happy.

A second knock ripped me from my thoughts, and I continued toward the front door. When I threw it open, my smile grew. There she was.

Her beautiful red lips were spread into a broad smile, and her stunning blue eyes were a different shade than they had been the day prior. Before, they almost matched the aquamarine lake I took her to. But, as she stood on my porch that morning, they were closer to crystal. Her hair was pulled into a high ponytail to keep it out of her face, but even up, it reached her shoulders. One section of her side-swept bangs hung down into her eyes, and every time she tried to move it back, it would drop right back down a few moments later.

"Good morning, sunshine!" Anevae said, snapping me out of the moment.

A small laugh slipped past my lips, and I smiled. "Good morning. Um, as you may be able to tell," I said as I gestured up and down at myself, "I am nowhere near ready yet. Please come in."

Anevae shuffled inside, and I closed the door behind her. When we got to the living room, I motioned to the couch. "Please have a seat while I get my life together."

Shaking her head, she huffed out a laugh and sat, waiting patiently for me. I ran around the house like a mad woman, trying to get myself ready. When I finally returned to the living room, she was playing on her phone. Walking past her, I dropped my backpack by the door and grabbed my boots so I could sit on the couch to lace them up.

"Where are we headed today?" she asked, looking up from her phone.

"That's for me to know and for you to find out," I said with a smirk.

"Well, that's no fun."

"It's not for you, but it most certainly is for me," I teased.

When I was done, I retrieved my backpack, and we headed out. I led Anevae in the opposite direction of where we'd ventured the day before. As we wandered into the trees, Anevae gazed around her, taking everything in.

"So, why did you choose to become a biological engineer?" I asked.

"Well, I've always loved being outside in nature. And I found out at a young age that I have a green thumb. My mom and I used to plant flowers and herbs when I was a kid, and I loved watching them grow. As a biological engineer, I've learned how I can impact our planet in both good and bad ways."

"Good and bad ways?"

She continued analyzing our surroundings and answered, "Yes. Have you ever heard of GMOs?"

"I can't say that I have."

"Okay, so GMOs are genetically modified organisms. Basically, a scientist brings a specimen, like a plant, into a lab where they try to modify the specimen's genetics so a desired trait is expressed. I know that sounds complicated, but let me explain."

Stopping for a moment, she stooped down and plucked a dandelion from the ground. "You see this, right? Imagine it's a yellow daisy."

After I nodded, she scooped down and picked up another dandelion. "Now, I want you to imagine that this is a blue daisy. If they were to produce an 'offspring,' we could possibly get yellow, blue, or maybe even green—it all depends on how they express that specific gene. Since I've never worked with 'daisies,' I wouldn't know, but a biological engineer will work with specimens to give them a desired trait. Working in agriculture, I've done a lot of experiments trying to get higher crop output, better temperature resistance, and more." She dropped the dandelions back onto the ground when she was done explaining.

"That's incredible. How does this position with Vision for the Future fit into that, though?"

"I'm not completely sure yet. I'm starting with these experiments to make sure nothing goes wrong, and the additive doesn't cause any modifications. It's definitely a big change, but I think it's something I really needed. I needed the space—the peace these woods can provide."

"Aren't you worried about being so far from your family?"

She stopped for a moment and looked at me. "I like to be alone. I've always felt like no one understood me or cared to try. I love my family and will miss my parents, but Eiri is in Havenridge. It's not that far. I don't like the hustle and bustle of busy streets and the loud noises always surrounding you. Even small towns have a little bit of it. I've known for a long time that I'd never be truly happy in a city with so many people nearby."

"I understand those feelings all too well. It was always busy where I grew up, and it felt like no one even remembered I existed until they needed something from me," I said sympathetically. Then, I looked into her eyes, and the blue depths threatened to consume me. "I hope you know that I enjoy spending time with you, and I do see you—I see you for the person you truly are. Even though you don't know me well, you've shown me such kindness. Many people wouldn't even bother. The neighbors I've had over the years have *never* come to introduce themselves to me."

Anevae took a few steps closer and placed her hand on my shoulder. She opened her mouth to speak, but nothing came out. After taking a deep breath, she tried again. "Thank you, Maeyve. That was very sweet. And I see you, too. You've been nothing but polite and uplifting since we've met. I appreciate how helpful and welcoming you've been. Yesterday's outing and the information you gave me has already helped me tremendously. These woods make me feel at home, and having you around gives me a sense of peace."

We stood there, lost in each other's eyes. When she pulled her hand away, I instantly missed the contact. We continued our trek in a comfortable silence. As we walked, I occasionally glanced over at her; I loved watching her. She was so intrigued by everything we saw, and I noticed the closer we got to the water, the more interested she became. I followed her gaze, looking down toward the creek, and was stunned by its beauty. The little details hadn't mattered in the past, but now, trying to see the world through her eyes, everything was brighter. I was fascinated by this woman and her desire to understand the world around her.

The roar of rushing water became overwhelming as we approached our destination—a waterfall I discovered several years prior. The creek we followed was a small fingerling of the river that led to the waterfall. When I first found it, I instantly fell in love, visiting often during the spring and summer. It wasn't an area that could be driven to, so the weather usually made it challenging to adventure to during the fall and winter.

As soon as it came into view, Anevae stopped to bask in its beauty. I couldn't help but watch her with the same reverence. The sun shone through the trees directly onto her beautiful hair, making the silky strands shine like a blazing fire. Her pale skin was rosy from our time in the sun as we followed the creek, and her mouth was agape as she took in the totality of the landscape before her.

Grasping her hand, I pulled her toward the waterfall. That tingling shot up my arm, causing goosebumps to appear on my skin. Anevae was still too focused on the scene in front of us to notice my reaction, but I saw a shiver go through her body at the same time. *Is she feeling the same thing I am?*

As we approached the water's edge, droplets strayed from the waterfall and crashed down on us. The cool water felt pleasant against my sun-warmed skin. Hand-in-hand, I led her to a nearby tree and slid my backpack off before setting it on the ground.

"I want to show you something, but you're going to get pretty wet," I said with a wink.

Anevae laughed nervously as she looked down at her clothes. Her light pink shirt would almost certainly become see-through when wet. With slight hesitation, she removed her backpack and placed it beside mine.

When she looked back up at me, I pulled her toward the waterfall. At the base was a rock wall with an edge wide enough to walk on. Letting go of her hand, I placed my hands on the wall in front of me to keep my balance. I started scooting slowly along the edge, holding on tightly to the slick, cold wall. The closer we got to the water, the more it sprayed us.

After a few more steps, the wall dipped in, revealing a large cave hidden by the water. As Anevae took her last step on the narrow wall, I pulled her away from the water to keep her from getting completely soaked.

"Thank you," she said breathlessly as she glanced around. The cave was full of rocks and sprouts of grass here and there, but moss from the waterfall's constant humidity was all over. A sheen of water covered the walls and greenery. Turning to the waterfall, she reached to stick her hand beneath the rushing water.

"Be careful. That water is extremely forceful and could easily pull you into the river. There's still quite a bit of snow from the peaks melting, so I'm sure it's pretty chilly in there, too," I said.

Anevae giggled and gave me a look of defiance as her hand slid into the water. I shook my head as she stepped closer to the fall. With her eyes still on me, she misjudged how close she was to the edge and stepped right into the water.

Shocked, I quickly dove in after her, cold water encasing my once-warm body. The waterfall's powerful flow forced me under, and I began paddling to get myself out. Surfacing, I looked around frantically for Anevae. When I didn't spot her right away, I began to panic, so I swam back down, spotting her near the bottom; the current of the massive fall was forcing her beneath the surface. As I swam closer, I began to be sucked in, but I was able to get away. I swam back and forth, trying two more times to retrieve her. On my fourth attempt, I grasped her wrist. With burning lungs, I kicked my legs as hard as I could, pulling us back to the surface.

Sucking in air, I clung onto Anevae, her body limp in my arms. I dragged her to the water's edge, where it was shallow, lifted her out, and deposited her on the grass. Climbing out, I checked for a pulse. It was thready and weak but still there, so I rolled her onto her side and began pounding on her back to expel the water from her lungs.

After several strikes, she began sputtering and coughing. Her hands flailed as she woke, and I quickly pulled her to me, cradling her in my arms. Her pulse raced under my hands, but as the coughing calmed, she began to shiver.

"It's okay, Anevae. I've got you. You're okay. Just breathe," I whispered in her ear.

As her shivering ceased, she pushed away from me, and I released her from my grip. She lifted her light blue eyes to mine. Now bloodshot from the underwater struggle, they were even more vibrant. Her quivering lips looked even more red against her cold, pallid skin. As a light breeze picked up, she wrapped her arms around herself.

Looking up at me through her lashes, she murmured, "I guess I should have listened when you told me to be careful." Blushing, she looked back down to the ground in front of her.

I lifted my hand to caress her cheek, urging her to look at me. "It's okay. I'm just glad you're okay. I got scared for a minute there."

Giving me a sad smile, she whispered, "Thank you for saving me."

As I stared into her beautiful eyes, I dropped my hand. I wanted to pull her into my arms and never let her go again, especially if that meant she was safe. Having her so close felt comforting, but I scooted back to put some space between us. I wanted her to be comfortable, and I didn't want to push her too far.

A look I couldn't discern crossed her face, and then she closed the distance between us. Her lips were on mine, her arms wrapped around my neck. The force of the kiss almost knocked me over onto my back, but her fingers tangled in my hair, keeping me upright. Once the shock wore off, I wrapped my arms around her waist and pulled her onto my lap, deepening the kiss. Her lips parted, and she slid her tongue out, requesting access to my mouth. When I parted my lips, her tongue darted in to caress mine.

We remained like that for several minutes, lost in each other. Then, she pulled back and slid off my lap to sit beside me. But before she could settle, I shot to my feet and began pacing. There was an intense throbbing in my clit that would continue to intensify if I didn't put some distance between us.

When the throbbing settled to a bearable level, I looked back at her. She was staring down at her hands with tears welling in her eyes. I rushed to kneel in front of her and explain, but she raised her hand to stop me from speaking.

"It's okay. You don't need to explain yourself. I'm sorry. I was too wrapped up in the moment. I'll keep my hands to myself from now on."

Before she could lower her hand, I grasped it and brought her knuckles to my lips, lightly kissing them. "I know you don't want an explanation, but I need to apologize. I, uh, I haven't kissed anyone in a long time. I just got a little nervous, and you're just so...perfect. And I'm not."

Blushing deeper, she shoved herself off the ground and darted toward her bag, trying to cover herself. Her light pink shirt had become completely see-through, and her white bra was visible. With her back to me, she yanked her jacket out of her pack, ripped her shirt off, and shoved her arms into the jacket, quickly zipping it up.

Turning back to me, she crossed her hands over her chest. "I'd like to go home now. Please. This has been beautiful, but I'd really appreciate some dry clothes."

Getting to my feet, I retrieved my bag and nodded. "Let's get you home."

There was an awkward silence as we walked back. When we approached, she headed straight for her car. *Was she seriously going to leave without saying anything?*

"I'm sorry about today," I blurted out behind her.

After she threw her backpack in the passenger seat, she turned to me, eyes darkened in anger. "There's *no* reason for you to be sorry. *I* was the idiot who didn't listen. *You* jumped in to save *me,* remember? If anything, I should be the one to apologize for being careless."

"Hey. It's okay. It happens. What matters most is that you're safe. Go home, get some dry clothes on, and relax. You need it."

"Thank you... Would you like to come to my place tomorrow? I'd like your opinion on how to best keep the animals away from my experiments."

"I'd love to. Why don't I come over sometime in the late morning, and we can go from there? You need to rest a little bit. You've done a lot over the last week."

"Sounds great. I'll, uh, see you tomorrow then."

I nodded. "See you tomorrow. Get some rest."

Then, she climbed into her SUV and went on her way. *Was there any way I could've fucked that up worse?*

I hurried inside, stripped off my wet clothes, and rushed out the back door. I couldn't bear to be away from her. I needed her like I needed water; I couldn't live without her. *Fuck. I'm in trouble.*

# Chapter Eleven

## Anevae

I woke the following day to the warm sun streaming in through my window. I rolled over to go back to sleep, but then my eyes snapped open. Maeyve was coming over! After the incident at the falls, I had been so exhausted that I forgot to plug in my phone. Cursing under my breath, I plugged it in and headed to the bathroom. When I was done, I tried to check the time again. 10:15 a.m. *Shit.*

Although we didn't set a specific time for her to come over, I knew we had agreed on late morning. Rushing back into the bathroom, I got ready and tried to be at least somewhat presentable. As I brushed my hair, there was a knock on the front door. I hurried to my bedroom, not paying attention to what I was wearing, and picked my phone up from the dresser. Yanking the charger from the wall, I sprinted down the stairs.

Standing on the other side was Maeyve. She was wearing all black again, which seemed to be her norm at this point. Her tight shirt accentuated all of her curves, and I couldn't help but stare until she cleared her throat.

I blushed deeply and held up my phone as I stammered, "I... Um, I'm sorry. Good morning. I didn't charge my phone last night, so I may have overslept just a little bit."

Giggling, Maeyve skimmed her eyes over my body and bit her lip before smirking. "Good morning to you as well. And it's okay. I tend to have that effect on some people. I'm not complaining about the view you're giving me, either."

My mouth popped open as I crossed my arms over my chest, trying to hide myself. Since I had rushed to answer the door, I hadn't changed out of my pajamas—a spaghetti strap tank top and soft fleece pants. My pierced nipples stood out from the cold air coming through the open doorway. I cleared my throat and stepped aside, "Please come in. Have you eaten breakfast yet? I also have coffee if you're interested."

"I ate a little before I came over, but coffee sounds amazing," she said as she entered the cabin.

My heart beat rapidly as I closed the door behind her. I took a few breaths, willing my heart to calm down. The scent of vanilla and berries filled my nostrils, reminding me of the first time I visited her house. She smelled so good.

I quickly stepped past her, leading her to the kitchen. She'd seen enough now, so I had no reason to change anymore; it wasn't like I was naked. She took a seat at the island while I brewed coffee for us. When it was ready, I took her a mug along with some cream and sugar in case she wanted it.

Moving to the fridge, I turned to Maeyve again, "Are you sure you don't want anything to eat? I don't have much to offer, but I have a few things. I really need to go to the store tomorrow."

"Thank you for the offer, but I think I'm okay with the coffee for now," she said, flashing a bright smile.

Grinning back, I grabbed the last of the eggs and some sausage links to make my breakfast before taking a seat across the island from her. I was nervous about sitting in front of her after she'd caught me staring at her. Deep down, I knew it was rude, but I couldn't help myself; I never wanted to take my eyes off her. *What the hell is wrong with me?*

I'd always been attracted to both men and women, but I'd never been in a relationship with a woman out of fear my family would disapprove. Something about Maeyve made me not care what my family thought, though. Chancing a glance at her, she was already staring at me.

"What's going through your mind?" she asked with a glint in her eyes and a sultry undertone in her voice. She had already finished her coffee but was still holding onto the mug.

Chuckling, I met her gaze. The orange of her beautiful doe eyes had intensified, and I could instantly feel my cheeks flush. "Well, honestly, I have a lot on my mind."

Her tongue swiped across her bottom lip as she set her mug down and stood up from her chair. Slowly, she stalked around the island to where I sat. I dropped my fork onto my now-empty plate and turned toward her as she approached. Sitting on the bar stool, we were at eye level as she strode to me. Seductively, she grinned and reached to separate my knees so she could situate her perfect, pear-shaped body closer to my center. She reached up with her dainty hand, caressing my cheek as she ran her thumb over my bottom lip.

Her grin turned to a smirk as she murmured, "I can't get that kiss yesterday off my mind—the feeling of your lips on mine. Your touch makes me feel like I'm alive for the first time in a long time. You're so breathtaking, and I don't want to keep my hands to myself anymore."

I bit my piercing briefly before whispering, "Then don't. Touch me, Maeyve."

Within seconds, her soft lips were on mine, and her scent engulfed me. My hands found her hips, pulling her in closer. She bit my lip, and I moaned softly. Her fingers tangled in my hair, pulling my head back to separate us. After kissing the corner of my mouth, she trailed kisses down my jaw to my neck. The dull thrumming in my center intensified as she got lower and lower. I wanted her to kiss me everywhere with those soft lips.

When she reached the top of my shirt, she whispered against my skin, "I've wanted you from the moment I laid eyes on you."

Relaxing my grip, I said, "I've thought of you constantly since we met. I look forward to every time I get to see you because being with you feels so natural. When you touch me, it feels like my skin is alive, and I never want you to stop. I don't know what's happening to me."

Without warning, she released my hair and stood back to look into my eyes. I was worried that I said something wrong. My worries were misplaced, however. She lifted me onto the island in a matter of seconds, and our lips collided again. Her hands slid up my hips and skimmed just under the hem of my shirt, eliciting a soft moan from me again. I needed to feel her skin against mine. Sliding my hand around to the base of her neck, I firmly grasped a handful of her jet-black curls. When our lips separated, Maeyve smiled and let out a soft sigh.

As soon as my lips met her neck, she gasped and gripped my sides tightly. I continued, and she moaned my name. *Fuck. How is she so perfect?* My clit began throbbing, and I loosened my grip on her hair. I wanted nothing more than to hear her say my name as I made her come over and over again.

With a giggle, she released my sides and removed my shirt in one swift movement. She tossed it onto the kitchen floor and took a small step back to look me over.

Instinctively, I reached up to cover myself, and her brow furrowed. "Please don't do that. I want to admire the beautiful woman in front of me."

Hesitantly, I lowered my hands, placing them on the island beside me, which made my chest puff out. Maeyve bit the inside of her cheek and stepped forward again. Reaching one hand up, she caressed my breast and swept a finger over my pierced nipple. I inhaled sharply—they were overly sensitive since I'd gotten them pierced a few years prior. Her eyes hooded as she slowly lowered her mouth to my breast, sucking my nipple into her mouth, and gently played with the piercing.

Throwing my head back, I reached up and grasped Maeyve's shoulder. She looped her free hand around my back to help support me. When she was done teasing one nipple, she moved on to the other. I grasped her shoulder tighter as pleasure rippled through my body. Releasing the hardened peak with an audible pop, she trailed kisses lower, easing me onto my back. The granite of the countertop was a cool contrast to the heat I felt within. When she reached the front of my pajama pants, she pulled the strings loose and deposited them on the floor. My bright pink, lace cheeky panties were the only piece of clothing left.

I tried to cover myself again, but when she noticed, she eased my hands away and tsked, waggling her finger at me. "You're beautiful just the way you are. Don't feel like you need to cover your body in front of me."

I had never felt comfortable with my body; I'd always been overweight. It made it difficult to find potential partners or anyone willing to look at me below my face. The way Maeyve admired my body amazed me. No one had ever looked at me that way. Ever. But she looked at me like I was some sort of goddess.

Her scorching gaze trailed over my body; then she slid her hand up the inside of my thigh. The feather-light tingling sensation that radiated through my body had me arching my back, anticipating where her hands would reach next. When she reached my panties, she played along the edges before slipping them off as well. Then, she bent down, placed her lips on my knee, and trailed kisses up my thigh as she spread my legs. When she met resistance, she stopped, looking up at me through her lashes.

"Open those legs for me, Anevae," she said, her voice husky with need.

When I didn't comply, she stood and met my gaze. "Is this too much for you?"

"No. Um, this is just my first time being with a woman, so I'm a little nervous," I murmured, lowering my head and covering my eyes. As soon as the words slipped past my lips, I felt stupid for saying them.

Maeyve stopped, bolting upright. "I'm sorry. I had no idea."

After pulling me back up, she started searching frantically for my clothes. I grabbed her hand to draw her attention back to me. "It's okay. I'm sorry. I didn't want you to stop; I just wanted you to know. I'm enjoying this a lot, so don't be sorry. Please."

Her brows were furrowed, and her eyes droopy as she turned back to me. "Let me make this a little more pleasant for you," she said, kissing me lightly on the cheek. I wasn't able to respond before she scooped me off the counter and headed for the stairs. She carried me as if I hardly weighed anything. Once we reached my bedroom, I pushed the door open.

She laid me on my king-size bed, and I closed my eyes. *Fuck. Did I mess something up? What is she doing?* I took a deep breath as I heard Maeyve shuffle toward the foot of the bed. *Damn it. Please don't leave.*

When I opened my eyes, Maeyve stood at the foot of the bed. "We can stop if you're not ready. I won't push you to do anything you don't want to do."

Shifting onto my knees, I crawled to the edge of the bed, directly in front of her. Reaching up, I placed my hands on her shoulders and pulled her to me. "As I said, I didn't want to stop downstairs; I just wanted you to know I've never done this before, so I'm a little nervous. I don't want to disappoint you either."

With a sigh, she pushed me onto my back and positioned herself between my legs. "I don't think you'd ever be able to disappoint me," she whispered against my skin. Her soft lips trailed down my body, finding my center. When she tried to spread my legs this time, I let her. She kissed a blazing trail down to my bikini line, and then she moved onto my knee, kissing a trail up the inside of my thigh. The closer she got to my throbbing pussy, the more I panted in anticipation.

Just when I started to settle down, she bit my thigh lightly. I gasped in shock at the delightful feeling and opened my legs even wider. Her teeth quickly released my thigh, and she licked a path straight toward my center.

She glanced up at me again and asked, "Are you ready?" As she waited for me to reply, she kissed my thigh again.

The only sound I got out was a whimper as I arched my back. I didn't want to wait any longer for her to touch me.

Without any additional warning, her mouth descended onto my pussy, licking up my wet slit. Then, she circled my clit with her tongue before sucking it into her mouth and releasing it. I screamed as a new kind of heat built in my core. No man I'd been with had ever gone down on me.

Sliding two fingers into me, I whimpered, "Holy fuck." She curled them up, searching for the perfect spot. "Oh my god! Don't stop. Fuck that feels so good."

She gripped me tighter and applied more pressure to my clit with her tongue. My screams grew louder the closer I got to climaxing. I wrapped my legs around her head to keep her from pulling away; I was already so close, and if she lifted her head for even a second, we'd be back to square one.

When I screamed my release, she continued her pursuit until my shaking ceased. I'd never felt pleasure so intense in my life. I unwound my legs from her neck and relaxed into the bed, trying desperately to catch my breath.

She crawled up the mattress and lay beside me, smiling and licking her lips. "You taste divine. I've never tasted anyone as delicious as you."

Blushing, I flipped onto my side to face her, "Thank you for making my first time unforgettable." Reaching over, I caressed her cheek and lightly kissed her soft lips again, slipping my tongue between them to taste myself on her.

As I started to trail my hand down her neck to her chest, she stopped me. "Not right now. This time was about you. We can worry about me another time. As much as I'd love to lay in this bed with you all day, we should get this day going."

I looked at her and stuck out my bottom lip, pouting. After shaking her head, I jumped out of bed and hurried into the bathroom to shower and get dressed. Maeyve sat on my bed, patiently waiting for me. About twenty minutes later, I walked back into my bedroom, ready to conquer the day. Smiling at Maeyve, I grabbed her hand and dragged her downstairs.

Entering the kitchen, I pointed at the island. "Sit. We need to figure out what we're starting with when we get out there."

Throwing up her hands, she huffed out a laugh. "Yes, boss."

Before sitting down, I grabbed a couple of glasses of water. I then explained the layout of my land and where all of my garden plots were.

After we formulated our plan, I looked at her playfully and asked, "Are you sure you don't want to finish what we started instead?"

She looked at me with a smile and shook her head. "Not right now. We have things to do."

"It can't be fair for you to pleasure me and not receive anything in return," I argued.

Leaning closer, she said, "Giving you pleasure was pleasing enough to me right now."

"Ugh. Fine," I grumbled. "If we're not allowed to have more fun in my bedroom, I guess we can go have some fun outside."

We explored the land until just before sunset. I gathered samples and jotted down notes about everything Maeyve told me. I didn't own any flashlights, so once it got dark, we headed back inside. Maeyve grabbed my hand to keep me close as we walked. The warm, tingling sensation was becoming a comfort, urging me to touch her.

As we entered the front door, we slid off our shoes and headed to the kitchen to grab dinner. After I heated the food – some leftovers from the day before – we took our seats across the island from each other again. Maeyve and I stole several glances at each other while we ate. Every time I caught her looking up through her lashes at me, the pulsing in my core amped up. All I could think about was how she had me splayed across the island earlier in the day.

"If you don't stop thinking about this morning, we'll end up with you naked on this counter again," Maeyve said with a smirk.

Giggling, I looked up at her through my lashes, attempting to be seductive. "Am I making it that obvious? What if that's exactly what I want, though? Except I want you to be the one splayed on the counter instead of me. I have several other areas around the house we could explore, but I'm always partial to the bedroom. I can be a pillow princess sometimes."

Maeyve's cheeks flushed, but her smirk deepened to a cat-like grin. "Hmm. Sounds tempting. I'd much rather take you on this counter again and have you scream my name repeatedly," she whispered.

Tsking, I got up from my seat and prowled around the counter toward her. "I think it's your turn."

As I approached, Maeyve turned toward me in her chair. Leaning in, I whispered, "As much as I'd like to show you around the house, I think I want a little bit of dessert first."

Stepping back, I grabbed her hand and pulled her up the stairs to my room again. When we reached the bed, I placed a quick kiss on her lips, then reached for her tight, black shirt. Drawing it over her head, I threw it onto the floor.

When she attempted to reach for my hips, I drew myself back and waggled my finger at her. "Uh-uh, Maeyve. Maybe when I'm done with you, but this is about you for now."

Reaching around her, I unclasped her bra and slid it off. Then I pushed her down onto her back and climbed on top of her. Straddling her, I leaned down and acted like I was going to kiss her but bit her lip instead. She gasped and grabbed my sides tightly. I proceeded to trail kisses down her jaw until I reached her neck and bit her again—her back arched underneath me as she moaned.

I licked where I had just bitten and sat up to look at her. "The sounds you make when I bite you make me want to do it over and over again."

Scooting down, I palmed one of her breasts and ran my thumb over her nipple. Maeyve bit her lip and stifled another moan.

Pinching her nipple, I scolded her, "I want to hear every sound that comes from that mouth." Bending down, I sucked her other nipple into my mouth and swirled my tongue around the hardened peak. She gasped and gripped the sheets. Refusing to leave the other side unattended, I gave it the same treatment. From there, I trailed kisses down toward her bikini line.

Sliding off her lap, I reached for her leggings and skimmed my fingertips just under the hem. She arched her back, and my heart began racing. The need I felt deep down to touch her—to feel her soft skin—amplified. When I pulled her leggings down over her thick thighs, I wanted to bite them to see how she'd react. With every intimate touch, kiss, and bite, she responded as if she hadn't been touched in a long time.

Kneeling between her spread legs, I trailed kisses from her knees to her panty line. Switching to the other side, I kissed halfway down toward her knee before biting her thigh. Maeyve's back arched as she screamed in pleasure.

"Oh my... That felt so good. Please do it again," she said breathlessly.

I licked the spot I bit and then did as she asked. Her reaction was the same as before, making me giggle. I licked the bite mark again and trailed my fingers up the outside of her thighs, reaching to pull off her panties. Once those were deposited onto the floor, I trailed kisses back up her body.

"Scoot up on the bed further. We wouldn't want you sliding off now, would we?" Maeyve complied without question. Smirking, I praised her, "Good girl."

Leaning over her, I ran my fingers over her belly's smooth, olive-toned skin to her bikini line. I slid my finger down her wet, warm center, eliciting another gasp. Teasingly, I ran my finger up and down several times.

Maeyve groaned and, through gritted teeth, said, "If you don't stop teasing me, I will gladly strip you instead and –"

I shut her up by sliding a finger inside of her and pressing my thumb to her clit. She gasped as I pumped in and out at a slow pace, trying to find the perfect spot to make her lose control.

Between moans, she whimpered, "Oh. My. God."

After a few more languid strokes, I added another finger and sped up my pace. She moaned louder, and her back arched off the bed. When her hand found my shoulder, she dug her long nails into it. My own pleasure surged deep down in me, and I let out a soft moan.

She continued to pant and gasp as I went, but I could tell this wasn't getting her close enough. Trying to increase her pleasure, I replaced my thumb with my tongue, slowly licking her clit. She cried out in pleasure and began shaking. Speeding up my tongue, she rode my face and fingers, finally finding her release. I continued to lap at her, sliding my fingers in and out until she cried out one last time. The sounds had ceased, but she lay there, legs shaking uncontrollably, sucking in deep breaths.

Pulling my fingers from her, I licked each one slowly, savoring the flavor of her arousal. Then, I licked up her slit again and hummed. When I lifted myself onto my elbows to glance up at her, she was already staring down at me, still trying to catch her breath.

She sighed and laughed. "Wow. Are you sure you haven't done this before? Because there's no way this was your first time pleasuring a woman. That was amazing!" she said as she sat up.

Smirking, I shifted onto my knees and reached out to pull her toward me. Once she got close enough, I kissed her deeply, and she slid her tongue into my mouth.

I bit her lip and then pulled back to look at her. "Let's go take a shower. I'd like to admire that body of yours a little more."

Crawling out of the bed, Maeyve followed me into the bathroom and helped undress me, planting kisses all over my body along the way. She was intoxicating. I didn't think I'd ever be able to get enough of her.

Once we were finished with the shower, I grabbed each of us a towel, and we got dressed. I extended an offer for her to stay the night, but she declined and said she had some things to take care of at home, so I walked her downstairs and saw her out.

# Chapter Twelve

# *Maeyve*

Before I left Anevae's cabin, I felt something I'd never felt before: I felt complete. The second I walked out the door, there was a tugging in my chest, as though one of my pieces existed only within her, and the further away I got, the less whole I felt. All I wanted was to feel her skin against mine for the rest of my life. *Did she feel the same way? I hoped like hell she did.*

My mind flashed with images of her skin on mine, followed by thoughts of that perfect body. It had been a long time since I'd been intimate with anyone, but no one could ever compare to her. If she would have let me, I would have worshiped her body all day and night. I shook my head, trying to clear it. If I kept this up, I would march right back up to her house and never leave again.

I wandered down to the end of the driveway so I could shift and look over the land more in my fox form. If I shifted too close to her home, I risked being seen. I was paranoid that she'd find me out when I wasn't ready. I was afraid of her reaction and couldn't bear the thought of not being near her if it went bad.

Reaching her mailbox, I undressed and stuffed my clothes into it. I wanted to keep them clean and dry in case it started raining. It was late spring, after all, and the weather tended to do weird things at a moment's notice. After I undressed, I got on my hands and knees, took a few deep breaths, and shifted.

After I felt the last bone settle into place, I wandered back into the woods to approach the ward again. As I drew closer, the ward shimmered lightly in the distance. Still apprehensive about stepping over the boundary, I approached it and halted, taking a moment to compose myself before I continued. I was still concerned something would happen even though she had permitted me to be there; I had crossed the barrier multiple times that day without repercussions.

When my nerves finally calmed, I picked up a paw to cross the boundary. As it reached the ground on the other side of the ward, I slowly followed suit with the other. When both paws were securely on the ground and there were no problems, I shook off the fear and trotted on, heading straight for the area where I'd found the ward's origin earlier in the day.

After Anevae invited me over, my biggest priority was investigating the ward. Then, I wanted to make sure nothing else had been tampered with on the property. As we walked through her property earlier in the day, we discussed the land and her plans for each garden plot. I enjoyed listening to her discuss her work; she was very passionate about it, and her dedication was evident in the thought she put into each of her experiments without even having started.

The first time I came to her property after she moved in, I spotted the origin of the ward on the eastern side of the cabin, which was magically inscribed into the ground and glamoured to the human eye. Anevae showed no indication that she could see it when we were out earlier; she didn't even seem to notice the ward surrounding her home at all.

The magic connected to the ward was a power so intense that I had no doubt a faerie from the royal family was the one to create it. My question then was, why? Why would a fae from the royal family be protecting this woman—whatever kind of being *she* was?

The inscription was written in the ancient language of Caellaias. I had no personal experience with the language, but I knew the royals were fluent in it. No amount of staring at it would magically decipher it for me. When I tried to focus on the identity of the being that sealed the ward, I could determine it was a shifter. Other than that, the glamour used to hide the inscription also muted the potency of the shifter's blood, at least to my senses; I couldn't tell what type of shifter had helped seal the ward.

When I was certain I couldn't glean any more information, I roamed the property to see if anything else was amiss. Grateful not to find anything else, I headed back to my clothes. I was tempted to return and accept Anevae's invitation to spend the night with her. But that was a bad idea. I needed to keep my space for the time being. I was already obsessed with her and didn't want to scare her off.

As I left her property, I was thankful for the ward. Being so close to the portal and not knowing anything about Caellaias, the ward protected her best. The portal wasn't easy to find by any means, but I'd seen lost beings come through it in the past. With the ward surrounding Anevae's home, she'd be more protected if a dangerous being came through. It made me feel more comfortable with her being alone.

Once I got to my cabin, I went inside and started getting ready for bed. The day had worn me out, and time couldn't pass fast enough before I saw Anevae again. I knew she needed to go to town for groceries the next day, and I was sure she would meet her sister while she was there.

Climbing into bed, Anevae was the only thing on my mind; I fell asleep with the memory of her skin touching mine.

# Chapter Thirteen

## *Anevae*

I woke up the following morning and went to the kitchen only to realize I had eaten the last of the eggs the day before. Without those, I couldn't figure out a substantial breakfast, so I texted Eiri to see if she was up.

Don't think so. I'm finally done unpacking, and my first interview is tomorrow, so I'm just relaxing. How about you?

I'm low on food, so I need to head into town today. Wanna grab breakfast and hit the store after?

Oooooooooh! Breakfast sounds amazing!

There's a cute little diner down the street called The Big Bacon Pancake. My neighbor told me they serve amazing breakfast!

We should try it! I'd love any chance I can get to spend time with my sister before she completely ditches me for her lame experiments.

I'm down!

Also, don't be a jerk because we chose two different career paths!

I love being outside. This job puts me the closest to the outdoors!

Anyway, I can meet you at the diner in thirty if I leave now. Send me the address. Thanks!

On the way to my car, I saw the black fox in the tree line. Stopping dead in my tracks, I stared at it. Bright orange eyes intently watched me. When I reached for my phone to take a picture, it took off in the opposite direction. Having missed my chance, I hopped in my car and headed to town.

About thirty minutes later, I pulled up to a charming little diner boasting all-day breakfast and the best pancakes in town. I didn't imagine that was hard to beat as the town's population was only about two thousand people, and there were only about three diners throughout. As I parked, I saw Eiri waiting by the door.

Walking up, I smiled at her and gave her a big hug. "I know it's only been a few days, but I still have missed you a lot," I whispered. Eiri and I hadn't been separated much growing up. Of course, we both went through our phases of wanting to be alone, but it never lasted long between us. We even went to the same college because we didn't want to be too far away from each other. While I loved my home in the woods, Eiri loved being near others, putting us a little further from each other than we were used to.

"Should we head inside? The hostess said there wouldn't be a wait when I checked in. The pancakes smelled AMAZING! I can't wait to try them," Eiri said.

"I'm always ready for pancakes! Let's get in there!"

As we walked into the diner, the scent of cooking pancakes and real maple syrup hit me, making my mouth water instantly; I just hoped the pancakes tasted as delectable as they smelled. The hostess showed us to a booth against the row of large windows at the front of the diner. She placed a menu in front of each of us before letting us know our waitress would be right over, and then she walked away. Once the waitress had collected our orders, we finally settled into some quiet conversation.

"So, have you started your experiments yet? Or are you too busy spending time with your neighbor?" Eiri asked, a teasing smile on her face.

I blushed just thinking about everything that was going on with Maeyve. "I haven't started any experiments yet, mainly because I'm waiting on the results of the soil samples I collected. I've been taking advantage of my downtime and spending some time with Maeyve. She's told me a lot of helpful stuff about the area. She's also really nice, and I enjoy spending time with her."

"Please be careful. You've only known her for a few days," Eiri said.

Feeling frustrated that Eiri wasn't trusting my instincts, I lowered my voice and chided her, "Eirian, I am a grown woman, and I trust my gut regarding her. You may not understand, but please try to cut me some slack. I know you just want what's best for me, and I appreciate that deeply, but please chill out with it already."

"Fine!" Eiri said harshly but continued, "I just don't want you to get hurt again. I know you've been interested in women, and it seems you're intrigued by her. I'm unsure why, as I haven't met her, but I can't watch you undergo another traumatic break-up."

Sighing, I looked down at my folded hands resting in my lap. "I know you're just concerned, but something is different about her. I will still be careful, but please don't say anything to our parents." Looking back up at her, I tried to change the subject. "Oh! Guess what I saw before I left the house!"

Eiri rolled her eyes, clearly not falling for it. "What did you see?"

"I saw the black fox! I've seen it more than once in the past couple of days, but it was right by the driveway when I walked to my car. It seemed like it was watching me. It darted away when I tried to take my phone out for a picture. Sorry, I couldn't get the picture for you. I'll keep trying," I promised.

Eiri stared at me as she seemed to think hard about what she would say next. "How about after the store, I come to your house? While I'm there, we can work on the greenhouse together, and you can show me around. When you showed us around the other day, we didn't see much, you know? Maybe I'll be able to see the fox with my own eyes."

"It would be nice to have you come over and spend some time with me. I'm sad we're so far away from each other, but I also love the area I've moved to."

When our food arrived, we chatted a bit more and ate. The pancakes were good, but I'd definitely had better. Before leaving, I paid the bill, and we made our way to the store. We pulled into the parking lot around the same time, exited our cars, and headed toward the store's entrance.

"What do you need? Did you bring a list?" Eiri asked.

"Of course I did." Pulling out my phone, I showed her the list on my notepad app. "Do you expect anything less from me?"

Eiri grinned. "I guess I shouldn't. We all know how meticulous you can be."

Putting my phone away, I strolled toward the store's entrance. Eiri fell right in line with me as she matched my stride. We perused the store for everything I needed plus some things I didn't. We decided to make that night a movie night, so we grabbed some ice cream and popcorn to enjoy during the movies we planned to watch.

When we were done, we loaded my car with the groceries I purchased and started the trek to my cabin. Eiri trailed me the entire way, still unfamiliar with the area. I had always been more comfortable with directions than my sister, so she relied on me or GPS for navigation. Unfortunately, GPS wouldn't get her directly to my cabin.

Pulling into the driveway, we parked side by side. Before going into the cabin, we each grabbed as much as we could, barely denting what was in my car. Three trips later, my kitchen island was full, and my car was empty.

It took us a lot longer than I liked to put everything away. I'd bought groceries and other necessities I didn't have for the house already, like decorations and towels for the guest bathroom upstairs. Glancing around, I sighed. Even with all the groceries I'd bought, the kitchen still looked barren. I didn't know having a colossal kitchen would be a blessing and a curse.

Satisfied with our work, we headed to the greenhouse. I was excited to decorate and organize it; having my sister by my side made things even better. She never understood my infatuation with nature but always supported me in any way she could, even if that meant doing something she didn't like.

Grabbing my speaker and phone, we got to work. My sponsors had given me enough supplies to get started with a few experiments and a large sum of money to purchase any additional supplies I desired. The amount they gave me both frightened and excited me. When I looked into the shops near the cabin that sold supplies for my experiments, I found that Havenridge didn't have any. That meant I would have to make a special trip to Fawnhaven if there were any additional supplies I needed.

Later, while we ate lunch, we discussed the plan for the rest of the day. Eiri again expressed an interest in venturing outside, as she'd only gotten a glimpse of the property when she and my parents helped me move into the cabin. Since I knew more about my land after spending time with Maeyve, I could give Eiri a more comprehensive tour of the area.

After we finished eating, we headed outside through the greenhouse. I started by showing Eiri the gardens around the property and explained how my experiments there would work during the late spring through early autumn. Because of how much snow the area historically received, I didn't want to do any experiments outside that would be affected by the extreme weather.

Eiri seemed interested in my work for the first time in years, asking several questions about how far out the garden plots went on the property. There were plots further into the woods where I could do some of my experiments, but I didn't plan on using them anytime soon. I wanted to start close by first.

When we finished looking around outside, the sun had almost set. I didn't want to be in the woods at night until I became more familiar with the area. As we headed inside, I spotted the black fox again. It seemed to be watching me from where it sat.

Catching Eiri by the arm, I pointed toward where the fox was and whispered, "Eiri, the fox is out there! Do you see it?"

She stopped dead in her tracks and looked toward where I was pointing. A bright smile spread across her face as she spotted it. "Oh my god. It's so pretty! I know you told me about it before, but seeing it with my own eyes, it's absolutely stunning!" She answered as she tried to reach for her back pocket.

As her hand descended, the fox took off into the woods. "Damn it! I really wanted a picture. Oh well. Maybe one day I'll be able to get one. You'll see me around here often if I get one of those work-from-home jobs now. I hope you have good Wi-Fi around here!" She said as she moseyed back to the cabin.

Shaking my head and laughing, I trailed after her. When we entered the cabin, I went to the kitchen to make our popcorn so we could have our movie night, and Eiri grabbed some soda from the fridge before sitting on the couch. After the popcorn was done popping, I grabbed a soda of my own and joined my sister to begin our evening of movies.

After a couple of movies, we both started nodding off and decided it was time to call it quits. Eiri had a job interview the next day and wanted to go home to prepare for it. When we were done tidying up the living room, we began saying our goodbyes.

"Hey, Vay? Do you mind if I hit the bathroom and grab a bottle of water before I head out?"

"Have at it. I'm going to bed... I'm beat. Oh, and lock the door on your way out, please."

"You got it. Have a good night, sis. Love you!"

Turning toward the stairs, I said, "Love you, too. Be careful on your way home."

"Okay, *mom.*"

"Just be glad I care, brat. I'm going upstairs. Do your thing and then get home. Good luck tomorrow."

About halfway up the flight, I'd already tripped on several stairs. *Holy shit. I hardly did anything today. Why the hell am I so tired?* I thought.

When I reached my room, I entirely skipped my bedtime routine because I was exhausted and crawled into bed. As I laid my head down, I heard the front door close behind my sister.

# Chapter Fourteen

# Maeyve

When I woke up, the first thing I did was check on Anevae. My dreams contained tidbits of my time with her the day before, so she was the only thing on my mind when I woke. Stripping myself of my clothing, I sprinted to the back door and went on my way.

As I crept up, she was walking out the door to her car. I was standing on the edge of the driveway when our eyes met. *Damn it. I need to start being more careful.* Once again, she reached for her phone to take a picture of me, and I took off in the other direction, returning to my cabin.

Once I returned to my cabin, I ate breakfast and got ready to drive into Fawnhaven. I needed to grab as many groceries as I could afford, and I wanted to check on Arturo.

His general store was situated on Fawnhaven's eastern edge near the woods, surrounded by smaller shops specializing in various goods. Many people visited the store because it had a wide variety of items ranging from trinkets and souvenirs to basic groceries like milk and deli meat.

Above the store was an apartment that Arturo and his family occupied. I'd only met his wife, Bernadette, and their son, Koda, a few times. Bernadette, also a bear shifter, was a sweet woman who loved her family with everything she had. She was fiercely protective of them and fought tooth and nail to be by Arturo's side.

Back in Caellaias, the couple's families were enemies, so when Bernadette and Arturo fell in love, their families threatened to separate them. To avoid that, they mated and fled to Earth. After successfully hiding themselves away, they settled into the general store and began trying to expand their family. It took them several decades to conceive Koda, but when they did, Bernadette was ecstatic. Koda was an adorable little boy—a perfect mix of his parents.

As I pulled up to Arturo's general store, I was startled to find that the windows and door were boarded up. My heart sank as I feared the worst had happened to them. Climbing out of my vehicle, I approached the shop to look around. When I looked through a gap in the boarded-up window, I saw the shop was empty of all goods; all that was left were the barren shelves. My stomach sank even further. Arturo would have never left his store like this unless something had happened to him or his family.

Moving to the door, I attempted to pull it open, and to my surprise, it was unlocked. I slipped inside, looking around to ensure no one saw me. Closing the door lightly behind me, I searched for clues about where Arturo and his family could have gone. I tried to look around but couldn't see much besides the empty shelves as it was too dark, so I turned to my other senses.

I closed my eyes and listened to everything around me. Above, I heard creaking in the floorboards. Was someone up there, or was the building just settling? My heart rate increased, adrenaline pumping. I hadn't brought any weapons—no means of protection. *Fuck. This is just great. If it's anything at all, I really hope it's Arturo or Bernadette up there.*

Taking a few steps toward the stairs at the back of the store, I sorted through the scents in the space. While I could detect many different kinds of food and drinks likely spilled on the floor, I could also smell the distinct scent of a bear shifter—a mixture of fish and pines. The smell intensified the closer I got to the stairs.

*Maybe it is still them upstairs. But why? Are they hiding from someone? Shit... Did one of their family members finally find them?* The possibility of finding the family dead plagued me, and a wave of nausea rolled through me.

Climbing the stairs slowly, I ran one hand along the old wooden railing and the other along the bumpy textured wall. The steep steps under me creaked harshly as I went. I tried to walk as tenderly as possible to avoid drawing additional attention, but one step creaked loudly when I was about three-quarters of the way up. Ahead of me, behind the closed door, a roar erupted. Then, loud footsteps came barreling toward me.

Sprinting up the rest of the stairs, I shoved open the door and came eye to eye with a large brown bear growling directly in my face. I threw my hands up and looked directly into its eyes. The bear's round, chocolate-brown eyes bore into me. My heart was pounding from the proximity of the bear and the angry look on its face. I willed my heart to slow along with my breathing. A glimpse of recognition flashed in the bear's eyes, and it relaxed. Slowly, it backed away and began shrinking, shifting back into the form of a human.

Before me stood a tall, naked, brawny woman, looking both frightened and relieved—Bernadette. She collapsed onto the floor and began sobbing. I rushed across the room and hugged her in a feeble attempt to console her.

"It's okay Bernadette. I just came to check on you guys. Where's Arturo? And Koda?" I asked, concern lacing my voice.

Between sobs, Bernadette responded, "Koda is in the back, sleeping. Artie left about a month ago but was supposed to be back in two weeks at most. He said we've been here too long, so it's time for us to move on."

Sadness came over me as she continued wailing and grasping me tightly. I hoped Arturo was okay for her sake. I stroked her long, brown hair to calm her. "He'll be back; I'm sure of it. Maybe it's been harder to find a place for you to go than he thought."

Bernadette nodded and took a deep breath. "I'm just scared, and we're getting kind of low on food. Koda eats a lot, and I'm with child again." Releasing me from her clutches, she leaned back. I hadn't noticed the small bump protruding from her lower abdomen when I first saw her.

"I'm so sorry, Bernadette. How far along are you, if you don't mind me asking?"

A small, sad smile spread across her face. "I'm about thirty-eight weeks, but you know how long shifter pregnancies tend to last."

Shifter pregnancies were the longest of the beings in Caellaias. They lasted at least twice as long as a human's pregnancy but also depended on the type of shifter. Bear shifters were large, and their pregnancies could last up to three times as long as a human's.

Just then, the store's front door slammed shut. Bernadette began growling and shifting back into her bear form as I moved aside. Before I could think to shift alongside her, there were steps fast approaching on the steps behind me. I turned to find a familiar figure rushing into the apartment. Arturo, a burly man of almost six and a half feet tall, looked frantically at his wife and then at me. Bernadette shifted back into her human form and hurried into Arturo's open arms as he started crying.

Arturo clung to his wife tightly. She was safe in his arms, and that gave him comfort. After a few minutes, he pulled back to look into her eyes. "I'm so sorry it's taken me so long to get back. I'm sure you've been worried sick, but I'm okay. How are you? The baby? Koda?" Moving one hand, he placed it onto Bernadette's swollen belly.

Bernadette smiled back at her husband. "We're all fine. We've just been worried about *you*. I'm so glad to have you back."

"I'm home now." After kissing his wife softly, Arturo's sad eyes drifted to me. "What are *you* doing here, Maeyve? When I saw your car outside and didn't recognize it, I started panicking because I knew it was just Bernie and Koda up here."

"I came into town to get groceries, so while I was here, I wanted to check on you guys. I was concerned when I saw the shop boarded up, but I pulled on the door, which just opened. Then, I heard movement up here and came to check it out."

Arturo looked back over to Bernadette and stroked her cheek. Sighing, he explained, "We have been in the area for too long now. I was out scouting and found a place with more shifters where we can blend in better. My family won't have to hide there; they are the most important thing to me, especially since we're growing again. I want to try this new place out and see how things go. If we decide to return, I'll still own this building."

"I'm just glad you guys are alright. I'll get going. Good luck to you all, and congratulations on the pregnancy," I responded sadly.

As I turned to leave, Arturo grabbed my arm, stopping me in my tracks. "I appreciate you coming to check on us. I know we weren't very close, but you've been great to work with over the years." Reaching into his pocket, he handed me a wad of cash. "I won't need all of this where we're headed. There's a whole community, and I have much more tucked away if needed. I won't be able to help you anymore, so I'd like to give this to you. Good luck, and take care of yourself out there."

Taking the money from Arturo, I whispered a teary thank you and rushed out of the building. As I got in the car, I stuffed the cash in my pocket and then headed further into town. There were grocery stores spread throughout the city, but I wanted to get in and out as quickly as possible. The first store I stopped at was too crowded, so I decided to skip that one and head for the next.

The parking lot of the next grocery store had fewer cars than the one prior. While it often meant the prices were higher, I didn't want to interact with more people than I already had to. Soon, that would have to change since I couldn't rely on Arturo for money or groceries anymore. About thirty minutes later, I left the store with my cart piled high, full of everything I'd need for the next few months.

Once I arrived home, I debated checking on Anevae again. I wasn't sure if she was home yet, but with the time I was away, it was hard to believe she wouldn't be. I hurried to put away my groceries, undressed in my bedroom, tossed my clothes into the hamper, and walked out onto my back porch. The sun was visible just above the treetops, slowly sinking behind them. The sky was just beginning to turn from beautiful baby blue to streaks of oranges and darker shades of blue.

Returning my gaze to the woods ahead of me, I shifted and sprinted toward Anevae's property. As I traveled up the tree line near her driveway, I saw a second vehicle next to hers. I assumed it was her sister's, but I'd never seen it, so I wasn't sure. Strolling on, I stayed behind the tree line, lurking in case they were outside.

Rounding the corner of the house, I spotted Anevae's bright red hair through the greenhouse windows. She reached for the door, and I paused as she exited with another woman in tow. I sucked in a sharp breath, finally able to compare them side by side.

I knew without question that the woman following Anevae was her sister. Her sister's hair and eyes were silver, like a shiny coin, drastically different from Anevae's, but their facial features were identical. They both had an upturned almond shape to their eyes, upturned button noses, high cheekbones, and full, lush lips. The most significant difference was that Anevae was a little shorter and had curves in all the right places, whereas her sister was taller and lanky.

I stayed just inside the cover of the woods, watching them stroll around. Anevae explained her plans for the property with her sister in great detail, which seemed odd. From my discussions with her, I'd gathered that her sister didn't seem to understand or be interested in her work or endeavors. Listening to their conversation, I noticed that her sister appeared eager to learn about her work and the property.

As they approached the cabin again, Anevae turned to stare directly at me. When she recognized my fox form, she quickly got her sister's attention and pointed me out. Then, her sister started reaching for her back pocket. Without another thought, I darted further into the woods the opposite way.

After running for about half a mile, I glanced back to make sure they hadn't followed me. When I didn't spot any movement, I took a moment to catch my breath. It was getting dark anyway. I was hopeful that Anevae and her sister had returned to the comfort and safety of Anevae's cabin.

As much as I wanted to check on Anevae, I didn't want to risk running into them again, so I wandered to the lake near my home for a quick swim. When I arrived, the sun had fully set, and the sky above was filled with millions of bright, twinkling stars. I admired the view for a while, searching for any constellations I could remember. I didn't know many, but I still enjoyed hunting for them.

When I had my fill of gazing at the stars, I searched for the moon. It was hanging low, just above the tops of the tall pines. Full and luminous, it reflected off the water before me. As I hopped into the cool water, the image became distorted.

I swam until my muscles ached and then climbed out into the brisk air, shaking off as much water as I could. On the trek back, I wandered through the meadow Anevae, and I had visited on our first day out, exploring the area together. It allowed time for my coat to dry a bit.

As I approached the meadow, I admired the gorgeous flowers that were just beginning to bloom. I'd always loved the flowers on Earth, but nothing compared to some of the varieties in Caellaias. One of my favorites was the orletaylaer. It looked like a teal rose but smelled like a sweet combination of vanilla and berries. Occasionally, I would wander near the portal to find some that managed to grow on Earth.

After admiring the meadow for a few minutes, I continued back to my cabin. As I walked up, I shifted back into my human form and went straight to the shower to wash off the lake water. Once I was done, I grabbed some pajamas and climbed into bed, falling asleep the second I closed my eyes.

# Chapter Fifteen

# Maeyve

I was awoken from my slumber by an intense magical pulse. I shot up from my bed and sprang into action, ripping my clothes off as I ran through the cabin. Reaching the back door, I shoved it open and raced into the pitch-black night, shifting into my fox form as soon as my bare feet hit the porch's wooden planks.

Landing just over the edge of the porch, I began stalking around the exterior of my home, searching for threats. While looking around, I tapped into my other senses to the best of my abilities; I was still groggy, making it difficult to determine where the pulses were coming from. No scents or sounds stood out among the floral notes and hooting owls.

When I made a full lap around the cabin, I established that there were no imminent threats to me. Focusing on the pulsing again, I began to move away from my cabin as I tried to figure out where it was coming from.

About a mile into my investigation, I heard a car speed past me on the dirt road. Scurrying closer but still trying to be safe and stay out of sight, I peered down the road. Unfortunately, I could only see the vehicle's tail lights before it disappeared altogether.

Trying to orient myself, I glanced down the road in the opposite direction and spotted a mailbox. Standing there staring at it momentarily, I realized where I was. Panic struck, and my heart rate quickened, finally making me more alert to the situation. Without another thought, I sprinted up the road to Anevae's driveway. I instantly knew something wasn't right; the ward around Anevae's home was gone.

Rushing up the driveway, I hurried to the inscription. As I approached, I could see that it had been mutilated; there were lines drawn through it, and it was covered in some sort of dark liquid that I couldn't distinguish until I got closer. The sour stench of a greater demon's blood hit me, and I realized it had been poured over the inscription. Demon blood was often used to neutralize magic, and everyone knew that the stronger the demon, the more potent the blood. Unfortunately, I knew that if I stayed too close to this blood, I wouldn't be able to smell anything else for hours.

Returning to the tree line, I scanned the ground for clues about who could have done this. Two sets of footprints led from the inscription; one veered to the left, toward the front of the house, while the other led into the woods. Of course, other older prints were scattered around, further from the inscription, likely from Anevae and her sister wandering the property earlier in the day.

I decided to follow the footprints into the woods to allow my olfactory system time to release the odor of the demon's blood. Trying to stay vigilant, I listened intently to the sounds around me. I could hear crickets chirping, a lone wolf howling, and snapping twigs. While I knew the twigs snapping could have been an animal, I still went on the defense. I refused to be ambushed.

As I crept through the woods, my nose reset, and an unfamiliar scent—leather and tarragon—invaded my senses. Stopping in my tracks, I deeply inhaled the intriguing aroma. Someone was nearby.

The prints I had been following headed in the same direction as the scent. Looking around, I recognized the area. Straight ahead of me was the portal into Caellaias. It was deep inside a steep mountainside cave several miles from our cabins. Mortals rarely found the cave. It wasn't nearly as challenging to find the portal entrance in Caellaias as it was in the mortal realm.

As I drew closer to the cave entrance, the scent grew stronger. Preparing for a confrontation, I tip-toed into the cave, carefully traversing the rocky floor and being mindful of where I placed my paws. The last thing I wanted was to cut one of them on the sharp rocks littering the cave's floor.

Just as I came around the last bend in the cave, a male figure disappeared into the shimmering portal. A frustrated growl erupted from my chest. I refused to follow him into Caellaias. Before leaving, I watched the portal for several minutes to ensure the mysterious being didn't return.

Once I was confident he wouldn't return, I headed back to my cabin. I needed to get dressed so I could check on Anevae. The sun was rising over the trees as I exited the cave. *How long has it been since I was roused from my sleep?*

When I returned home, I rushed into my bedroom and grabbed my phone. I texted Anevae, hoping she'd answer me, and then pulled on some clothes. After sending several texts with no response, I called her instead. When she didn't answer, I rushed out of the house, jumped in my car, and sped over to her cabin, praying she was okay.

# Chapter Sixteen

# Anevae

Heavy pounding woke me from a deep sleep, and confusion rolled over me as I tried to figure out where it was coming from. I rolled over and opened my eyes just as a wave of nausea overcame me. My head spun, and I felt disoriented and groggy. Closing my eyes again, I lay there for a couple more minutes, willing my stomach to calm, but the pounding continued. Once I felt a little better, I sat up. Looking toward the stairs, I heard the pounding continue again and realized where it was coming from. Someone was pounding on my front door. Why? Who could it be? Throwing the covers off, I stomped downstairs to check things out. To my surprise, Maeyve stood on the other side of the door, eyes wide, breathing heavily, and hair a mess.

"Oh, thank goodness. I was so worried about you!" she said, breathing a sigh of relief.

Still feeling quite groggy, I rubbed my eyes and glared at her. "Why on earth are you pounding on my door?" Peering around her, I noticed the sun was already pretty high in the sky. "Wait... What time is it?"

She cocked her head slightly as she answered, "It's just after 9 a.m. I've been knocking on the door for over half an hour. I was half tempted to break it down if you didn't answer in the next few minutes. Are you okay? Did you just wake up?"

As I listened to her talk, my head began spinning again. Closing my eyes, I covered them with one hand and held onto the door frame with the other. As I tried to breathe through it, I responded harsher than intended, "Yes, I just woke up. And I really don't feel that well right now. You still didn't answer my question as to why you've been pounding on my door."

"I tried texting you several times to see if you had plans for the day, and when you didn't answer, I tried calling you. After calling you multiple times with no answer, I had this horrible feeling, so I rushed to check on you. Seeing your car in the driveway scared me even more because it meant you were home. Did you not hear your phone?"

"I haven't heard my phone ring at all this morning!"

She shook her head and pointed at the stairs, "If you don't believe me, go get it." When I didn't move, she huffed and looked behind me. "Did you go to the store yesterday?"

"Um, yeah. I met my sister in town, and we went together. Why?"

Without a response, she strode into the house, heading straight for the kitchen. Slamming the door, I trailed her. "Where on earth are you going?"

As she turned to face me, her eyes glowed bright orange again. "You just woke up, so I know you haven't eaten yet. I want to make you something to eat. Is that okay?" she asked, her tone agitated.

My mouth fell open. "Um, you don't have to do that. I can make my own breakfast. I just need to get my phone to make sure I didn't miss anything else."

Maeyve's lips pursed as she clenched and unclenched her jaw.

Gesturing toward the kitchen, I said, "Okay. If you really want to make me breakfast, have at it. I'll be back in a few minutes." I turned around and wandered up the stairs to use the bathroom and grab my phone. *This has been a bizarre morning. Did she really call and text me multiple times? I don't think I've ever slept that heavily in my life.*

Sitting on my bed, I unlocked my phone. Sure enough, there were dozens of texts and missed calls from Maeyve. *Oh shit. She really was telling the truth... I need to apologize.*

While descending the stairs, I smelled one of my favorite breakfast foods: pancakes. Confused, I tried to remember what I'd bought at the store the day prior. I was confident I hadn't picked up any pancake or waffle mix, which meant she made the pancakes from scratch. My parents were the only ones who had ever made me homemade pancakes.

Coming up behind Maeyve, I wrapped my hands around her midsection. It had been a long time since someone other than my family and best friend had shown me such kindness, and I appreciated it more than I could express to her. Against her back, I whispered, "Thank you. I'm sorry I've acted like a raging bitch this morning. I'm not really a morning person, and I don't like to be woken up so abruptly."

She giggled when I planted a quick kiss on the back of her neck. Then she turned her head toward me. "I appreciate your apology, and you don't need to thank me. This is nothing."

Moving beside her, I twirled my thumbs and bit my lip piercing. "I just haven't had many people treat me so kindly—especially someone who's only known me for such a short amount of time. Even my ex-fiancé wouldn't have done something like this for me. Not to mention that I was a complete asshole to you this morning," I replied quietly.

Grasping my chin, she forced me to look up at her. "You deserve the world and more. Never let anyone make you feel like you don't." Before she returned to the food, she planted a firm kiss on my lips.

Grinning from ear to ear, I turned to brew some coffee for us. When it was done, I fixed my cup and left one for Maeyve on the counter with the fixings. I tried to ask if I could help her, but she refused, so I sat at the island, admiring the woman floating around my kitchen.

A few minutes later, Maeyve served me my breakfast and sat on the opposite side of the island with her plate. My stomach had finally settled, so I dug in. The pancakes were fluffy, buttery, and absolutely amazing. I wasted no time devouring them, not realizing how hungry I was.

Maeyve giggled as I glanced up at her. She was barely taking her second bite of food. Blushing deeply, I reached for my coffee and took a small sip. When she finished her food, she grabbed my plate and headed for the sink. I tried to convince her she didn't need to do the dishes because she cooked breakfast, but she stared me down and raised an eyebrow, insisting in her way that she was going to do them anyway.

While she washed the dishes, I stripped her of her jacket and deposited it on one of the barstools. Then, I placed kisses across her shoulder blades as she finished up. When she was done, she dried her hands and turned to face me. I looped my hands around her neck as her mouth descended onto mine, and she lifted me onto the island.

Unlocking our lips, I trailed kisses across her cheek to her ear, whispering, "Let's take this upstairs." Then, I bit her earlobe softly, and she sharply inhaled. Without warning, she lifted me off the island and carried me upstairs.

I giggled as she dropped me onto my bed. When our lips collided again, she slipped her hand under my shirt to my breast, where her thumb and index finger found my nipple. She pinched lightly, and I gasped as pleasure coursed through me straight to my throbbing clit. Then, she moved to the other side, giving it the same treatment.

When her lips left mine, she kissed along my jaw to my neck, where she bit me hard enough it would leave a mark. I moaned and gripped her shoulders, loving the feel of it. She huffed a breathy laugh and kissed down my neck until she reached my chest.

Climbing off the bed, she urged me to sit up with her and pulled my shirt over my head. Then, she gently pushed me onto my back, where she continued stripping me of my pants and underwear. Once again, I was completely naked in front of this stunning woman, and I tried to cover myself.

She wagged her finger and kissed back up my body. When she reached my neck, she leaned in close and whispered, "If you cover yourself again, you will receive a punishment. I want to see all of your beautiful body." As she sat up, she skimmed her hands over my skin. "These beautiful breasts, this smooth belly, those juicy thighs, and this pretty pussy—I want to claim every piece of you with my mouth and hands." As she slid her hand over my wet center, my back arched.

Her touch felt so good that I never wanted her to stop. I sprung to my feet and claimed her lips again, hungry for her kiss and touch. Reaching for her shirt, I yanked it over her head. She wasn't wearing a bra, making it easy for my hands to find her breasts and play with them. A small moan escaped her lips. Moving down, I slid her pants and underwear to the floor.

"I need you to understand that I've never been secure in my body. It's instinct for me to want to cover up. I'll try not to cover myself in front of you unless I want to feel what it's like to be punished," I explained with a smirk.

She smiled back at me, and I pushed her onto her back, moving to kiss up her body. In my past relationships, I'd always been submissive to the men I was with. For the first time, I wanted to be in control. *Would she let me dominate her?*

When I reached her breast, I sucked a nipple into my mouth, rolling it around on my tongue before biting it. Her back arched as she grabbed onto my side tightly, digging her sharp nails into my skin. Releasing her nipple, I continued further down. Reaching her bikini line, I moved down to spread her thighs.

Before I could, she stopped me. "Come up here. I want you to sit on my face while you play with me. You won't be able to use that delectable mouth the same way, but I'm positive it'll still be amazing no matter what."

I was nervous about doing as she asked. Being a bigger woman, I was afraid I would suffocate her, but she was insistent, so I moved to situate my pussy right above her face. I'd never done this before, so I tried to just hover over her mouth, but she grabbed my hips and pulled my warm, wet center onto her firm tongue. The contact had me moaning loudly. Her tongue swirled over my clit with expertise. For a moment, I couldn't focus on anything, but when she squeezed my hips, I remembered this wasn't just about me.

I skimmed my fingers down her side to the inside of her thighs. As I slid my fingers over her slick folds, she gripped my hips harder. Grazing my fingers up and down again, she stopped. I giggled as I placed a kiss on her belly and plunged two of my fingers into her. She gripped my thighs tighter, and her nails dug deeply into my flesh. I was sure she had broken skin this time, but to my surprise, pleasure coursed through me instead of pain. Moaning loudly again, she continued her pursuit while I plunged my fingers inside her as deep as I could. As I pumped them in and out, I felt the rigid spot I could only imagine was her G-spot and began rubbing it vigorously. The faster I moved my fingers, the faster she moved her tongue, and the tighter she gripped my hips. I felt my release building steadily until I couldn't hold on any longer and climaxed with a scream. With one last thrust of my fingers, Maeyve tumbled over the edge with me.

Exhausted, we flopped on the bed side by side.

"That. Was. Amazing," I panted.

She laughed breathlessly and moved to face me. Looking her dead in the eyes, I sucked on each of my wet fingers slowly, savoring the flavor of her arousal. She just stared at me, and for the first time since I'd met her, she looked at peace.

Relaxing again, I asked, "What are you thinking?"

She closed her eyes and smiled. "Just how beautiful and perfect you are. You're the most beautiful woman I've ever laid eyes on. How can you not see that? You're so kind and amazing to be around. How has no one snatched you up yet?"

Then, I laughed, trying to avoid answering the latter question. "I have a hard time seeing that about myself. I've always known I was pretty to some degree, but I'm overweight, and I've been bullied for it for the majority of my life."

The next thing I knew, I was on my back, and Maeyve was pinning me down, glaring at me. "I want to get one thing straight with you. I don't care how overweight you think you are; you're beautiful just the way you are. I wouldn't change a single thing about you, even if I could." When she finished speaking, she kissed me on the nose and let me go. Then she strolled to the bathroom, and I hurried to catch up.

Running the water in the tub, I held my hand under the stream until the temperature felt just right, then grabbed my bubbles and poured some in. I glanced at Maeyve, who was already bringing a towel and washcloth for each of us. I smiled, thanked her, and placed a quick kiss on her lips, which still tasted of me.

When the bathtub was full, I shut the water off, and we climbed in, sitting across from each other. As the water enveloped me, all the tight muscles I didn't realize I had relaxed. Letting out a sigh, I laid my head against the marble tub. Maeyve picked up one of my feet and began massaging it. I let out another soft sigh, and she giggled.

We sat there in comfortable silence as she massaged my feet and calves. Then, she grabbed a washcloth and my favorite soap and began washing me. She was gentle with every swipe of the cloth but made sure she didn't miss anything. After I was nice and clean, I grabbed the other washcloth, lathered it up, and did the same for her.

When we were both cleaned off, we took turns washing each other's hair. Maeyve massaged my scalp, and I was in heaven. I did the same when it was her turn, trying to massage her scalp as well as she had massaged mine. As I rinsed the conditioner from her hair, I realized how peaceful she looked again. I had a feeling no one had ever cared for her like this, either.

After our bath, I decided I didn't want to go outside anymore, so I put on some pajamas and found some I thought might fit Maeyve while she relaxed at my cabin. When we were comfortable, we wandered downstairs to find something to do. The first thing Maeyve saw was my movie collection, so we picked a few to have a movie marathon. While I went to the kitchen to make popcorn, I asked Maeyve to grab some blankets.

By the time the popcorn was prepared, Maeyve had already settled on the couch, found the remote, and got the first movie queued up. As I walked over, I placed the popcorn on one side of her and plopped down on the other side, cuddling up to her. We watched movie after movie until I fell asleep.

# Chapter Seventeen

# *Anevae*

I woke the next morning in my bed with no recollection of how I'd ended up there. The last thing I could recall was falling asleep on Maeyve's shoulder. I reached over to the other side of the bed to see if she was there, but it was unoccupied. As I sat up, she walked through the door with two plates and a couple of forks hanging from her mouth.

After she handed me a plate, she reached up and took the silverware out of her mouth, flashing a bright smile. "Good morning. You look so cute when you sleep. I didn't want to wake you." She kissed my forehead lightly, then handed me a fork and sat beside me on the bed.

I didn't realize how hungry I was until I smelled the omelet she made me. When I took my first bite, my eyes rolled back, and I let out a small moan. I wasn't sure what she put in the omelet, but it was delicious.

"Well, I'm glad to see I'll be able to make you moan outside of the bedroom as well," Maeyve said with a giggle.

Trying not to choke on my food, I swallowed and smacked her arm. "Wow! I wasn't expecting that from you! You already know you can make me moan anywhere you want."

In a matter of minutes, my omelet was gone. When we were both done eating, I placed our plates on one of the end tables and climbed back onto the bed in front of Maeyve.

Putting my finger on her lips, I purred, "Let me show you my appreciation." Then, I replaced my finger with my lips, kissing her long and slow. But before pulling back, I bit her lip, and she chuckled.

"I like where this is going," she whispered, eyes darkening as she looked at me.

Wetting her lips, she pulled me in for another kiss, and I skimmed my hands down her sides. When I found the hem of her borrowed shirt, I slid my fingers underneath to feel her smooth skin. Separating for a moment, I pulled the shirt over her head and pushed her onto her back.

Moving to straddle her, I admitted, "You know, I've never been given the opportunity to be in control during sex, but I'm finding that I like it sometimes. I love hearing all the sounds you make and knowing I'm the one causing you to make them."

Maeyve smiled and placed her hands on my hips. As she started talking, she ran her hands up and down my thighs, sending a heat wave through my core. "You can't have control all the time, sweetheart. Know that I feel the same way about pulling those delicious sounds from your lips. I'm finding that I kind of like letting you take over sometimes, though."

Leaning down, I whispered in her ear, "My question for you is, how much control are you willing to give to me?"

Her hands stopped when the last word slipped past my lips. I tried to sit up to look at her, but she gripped my hips and flipped us over so I was pinned beneath her. Lowering her mouth to my ear, she nipped at my earlobe. "One step at a time there, sweetheart. Just because I said I like letting you take control didn't mean I would give up all control right now."

As she started kissing down my neck, I said, "Well damn. I was just about to have a lot of fun."

When she reached my collarbone, she sat up and reached for my shirt to work on the buttons that adorned the front. After a few torturous seconds, her hands slid underneath the open fabric to the bare skin of my belly.

"You're so beautiful," she murmured as her eyes skimmed over my exposed skin.

Sitting me up, she removed my shirt. As I laid back down, her lips were on mine again. After several sensual and deep kisses, she trailed kisses down my neck, where she bit me playfully. Then, she licked the spot, sending more heat waves through my body.

I reached up and tightly held her shoulders as she descended lower. When she reached my chest, she licked a line to my nipple. Arching my back, she took the opportunity to pull the hardened peak into her mouth, biting it lightly. After releasing it, she played with the piercing. When I arched my back again, she moved to the other side, giving it the same treatment.

Lifting her head, she looked at me through her lashes and asked, "Do you like it when I bite you?" When I nodded, she planted a kiss on my sternum and gave me a sly grin. "Does it allow you to feel more pleasure?" When I nodded again, she let out a short laugh and trailed kisses back up to my neck.

Moving to sit up, she skimmed her hands across my skin. "I love how you react when I bite you; you make such beautiful sounds, and your pulse quickens every time. They say pain can induce pleasure. If you like biting, I wonder how much you'd like it if I spanked that juicy ass." When the last word left her lips, the pulsing in my center amped up, wishing she would do it.

A devious grin crossed Maeyve's face as I squirmed beneath her. "Have you ever been spanked before?" I chewed my lip ring as I shook my head. "Do you like the idea of being spanked?"

With another nod, I said, "I'd love to know what it feels like."

Maeyve's orange eyes lit up like a fire had been ignited behind her irises. She slid her fingertips under the hem of my shorts and stroked the sensitive flesh there. Then, she gripped my hips and flipped me over, lifting my ass into the air. She groaned as she pulled my shorts and panties down, discarding them on the floor.

My ass was still up in the air, and just the thought of her looking me over had wetness dripping from between my thighs. I glanced over my shoulder at her. She was sitting back on her haunches and had sucked her bottom lip into her mouth; her stare was locked onto my ass.

As I watched her, she raised her hand and brought it back down on my sensitive flesh. The sting of the impact shocked me at first, eliciting a gasp, but then my skin began to tingle, and I whimpered. The sensations sent a direct shot to my clit, and it throbbed. I wanted more. How would it feel to have her do it time and time again?

I'd experienced pain in the past when I was engaged to Ambrose, but never like this. His goal was to break me; Maeyve's goal was to bring me more pleasure. I'd dabbled in some BDSM during my hook-up phase after my engagement with Ambrose ended, but my relationship with him continuously haunted me. No matter how much I tried to avoid thinking about him, he always snuck in at the worst possible times.

Maeyve rubbed my ass in the spot where she hit, pulling me back into the moment. Then she arched her hand up and around, coming down on my ass again. I let out another whimper and flinched on instinct. When she shifted, I glanced back at her.

Her brows had furrowed, and her lips pursed before she asked, "What's wrong? Did I hurt you? Did I hit you too hard?"

Biting one of my lip piercings, I took a deep breath and lied, "I'm fine."

"You're not fine. You've got a death grip on the sheets, and you flinched when my hand made contact the last time. Please talk to me."

Turning around, I sat up on my haunches. The red-hot skin on my ass bumped up against my heel, and I winced. All thoughts of pleasure had been erased from my mind.

"I'm sorry. It's a very long story for another time, but I was hurt in a past relationship, and it still haunts me. I know you have no intent to hurt me the way he did, but it still plagues my mind at the worst possible times."

"I'm so sorry you had to go through that. I want you to know I would never hurt you intentionally. Where is this prick?" Maeyve asked.

"Well, I'm not sure what happened to him after our engagement was called off."

"I hope he got what he deserved. If anyone ever lays a hand on you again, I will waste no time in causing them ten times more pain than they ever could have thought to cause you."

Tears lined my lower lids. When the last words left her lips, I whispered, "I'm sorry."

"You don't need to apologize," she murmured, caressing my cheek. "Let's go downstairs and make some coffee so we can truly start the day."

After finishing our coffee, we headed upstairs again to get dressed. The weather was warm enough that I didn't need a jacket, and I was ecstatic. Autumn was my favorite season back home, but late spring here was beautiful so far. The mountains' temperatures drastically differed from those I was used to on the East Coast.

I pulled on a long-sleeved flannel and thick leggings while Maeyve put on the clothes she had worn the day before. Most of my clothes wouldn't fit her taller and leaner frame without falling off or being too short.

As Maeyve followed me through the greenhouse with an armload of supplies, she teased, "Aren't you glad I'm here to help? You would've had to make more than one trip to take everything outside." I turned to glare at her, but the grin plastered on her face made me smile instead. "Where are we starting today?"

"We're going to the plots on the edge of the woods so I can keep a close eye on everything from the greenhouse."

"Okay. Sounds like a plan. Please let me know how I can help you as we go. I'm interested in what you're doing and hate feeling useless."

"You're silly. I hope you realize you're the exact opposite of useless. I'll let you know if I need help, but I'll gladly have your company. I love spending time with you."

Her cheeks turned a bright red. "Thank you. It's been a long time since I've had company, and I enjoy being around you, too. Are you ready to head out?"

When I nodded, she opened the door for me, and we wandered out to the garden plots. The sun's warm rays danced over me. It was invigorating. However, the closer we got to the woods, the harder it became to feel the heat through the trees.

Once we reached our destination, I set down the items I was carrying, and Maeyve followed suit. Grabbing my tools, I began preparing the soil in both plots. One plot would include the soil additive, while the other would be untouched. Doing this allowed me to compare how well the increased amount of Manganese helped the plants grow. All the other components would be the same for each side: temperature, amount of water, and sunlight.

As I did my work, Maeyve sat on the ground, watching me, and asked several times if she could help me. Laughing every time she asked, I refused the help until I was ready to plant the seeds.

Pulling two seed packets from my pocket, I handed one to Maeyve. "These are tomato seeds. I want you to make shallow little holes about a quarter of an inch deep and keep them an inch apart, then put two seeds in each hole and lightly cover it."

"I can do that," she said and then set to work on the control side.

I watched her for a moment, appreciating the effort she put into this small thing that was so important to me. Refocusing on the task at hand, I made my small holes as I'd told Maeyve to do and added three drops of the additive to each one. Capping the bottle, I ripped open my packet and placed two seeds in each hole before covering them and leveling the ground. I'd see seedlings erupting from the soil in about a week, but it depended on how much the temperatures fluctuated. I was still excited. I loved seeing each plant's stages and how each was slightly different from the one next to it.

When I was done planting, I brushed my hands on my pants, shaking away the excess dirt. Looking over, I was surprised to find Maeyve staring up at me from her spot on the ground, already done with her task.

"You were fast." My voice was lighthearted as I added, "Did you do everything just how I told you to?"

Maeyve's mouth dropped open. "Are you saying I'm incompetent?" Standing up, she approached me with a smirk.

My cheeks reddened in embarrassment. "Th-that wasn't at all what I was trying to say!"

"I know you were just kidding. It was my turn to give you heck. I did *everything* just as you told me to. What else needs to be done out here?"

"I just need to water the plots and do some paperwork to document the start of my experiment. Other than that, I have no other plans right now."

Grabbing my hand, she pulled me to her and gave me a light kiss. "Let's take these tools inside and grab your watering cans. Then, we can eat lunch and figure out what to do from there. How does that sound?"

Pulling her knuckles to my lips, I gently kissed them. "That sounds like a great plan."

# Chapter Eighteen

## Maeyve

Upon our return to the cabin, the scent of leather and tarragon hit my nose. I held the door open for Anevae and lingered outside, searching for the source.

Anevae watched me with curiosity in her gaze but didn't comment as she stepped inside to find the watering cans. I continued sniffing at the air, on high alert for the intruder. By the time Anevae returned to me with the watering cans, I still hadn't located anything or anyone unusual.

She attempted to hand me one, but I took both watering cans from her. "Why don't you head inside? I can take these to the garden plots and water them *carefully* for you. I'll meet you back inside shortly."

"O-okay. Thank you." Her brow furrowed as I kissed her on the temple and stepped back toward the plots.

The scent was so faint that I had a hard time picking up on it. The other smells—the dirt on my hands, the grass beneath my feet, the pine trees surrounding the cabin—were all so much stronger that they drowned out the smell of the being.

On constant alert, I watered the plants precisely as Anevae had instructed and placed the cans aside. Glancing back toward the greenhouse, I saw that Anevae had gone inside the cabin itself. Relieved, I considered my options: chase down the source of the smell and leave Anevae here—alone and unprotected—or go inside and stand guard for the rest of the night. A twig snapped just inside the tree line as I stood there. Whipping my head toward the source of the sound, I caught the outline of a man about twenty feet ahead of me.

Without another thought, I ripped off my clothes and shifted into my fox form, sprinting into the woods after him. He was fast—so fast I struggled to keep up with him. I jumped over fallen trees and large rocks until we came to a clearing, where he abruptly stopped and turned to face me.

Skidding to a halt, I bared my teeth and growled at the man. He was fairly tall, a couple inches over six foot, lean and muscular. His chiseled face was mostly hidden by a short, well-groomed beard and his black hair had been slicked back but trimmed short on the sides. Hissing at me, his full lips pulled back to reveal gleaming white teeth and elongated sharp canines. He was a vampire, and he had his deep red eyes fixed on me. *Shit. What the hell was a vampire doing out here? Why was he running from me?*

"Hello, little fox. Maeyve, is it?" the vampire asked, cocking his head to the side.

I snarled. *How the fuck does he know my name? Who the fuck is this vampire?*

"Ooh. My suspicions were correct, and I struck a nerve. I've been watching you and trying to figure out who you are; now I know. Madam Tanith will be pleased to learn that her most prized possession is still alive."

Inching forward, I barked at him.

He laughed before continuing, "You seem a little infatuated with her, following her like some sort of love-sick puppy. It's pathetic. I hate to be the one to tell you this, little fox, but she's not yours to have. If you know what's best for you both, you'll leave her be. I'll gladly speak with Madam Tanith to tell her you're alive and well... In the human realm, nonetheless. Anyway, I better be going. This sun isn't good for my complexion. Buh-bye Maeyve."

Smirking, he darted in the direction of the portal. I followed him to make sure he returned to Caellaias and didn't come back. I sat there for several minutes, watching the portal and thinking about what he said. *What did he know about her? What did he know about* me? *How did he know about Madam Tanith?* I wouldn't go back there; I couldn't. It'd been over fifty years since I'd escaped her. I needed to figure out what kind of being Anevae was and why the damn vampire was watching us.

When I reached my clothes, they were soaking wet and covered in mud. *Shit.* Scooping them up, I went back into the woods so I could shift back into my human form. I shifted behind the cover of a tree and rushed back to the greenhouse.

Entering, I quietly closed the door behind me. After the soft click, I cracked open the cabin door and hollered, "Anevae, I've gotta run home to get some more clothes—the ones I was wearing got all wet and muddy. And, of course, I don't have any others here right now. I'll be back shortly."

"Oh no! I'm sorry. I hope I didn't fill the watering cans too full for you. I'll be here. I might run upstairs to document this experiment before I forget absolutely everything."

Closing the door, I went back outside and shifted again. I returned to where I'd left my clothes and picked them up to take home.

After my encounter with the vampire, I had no plans to leave Anevae alone. Fuck his threat of exposing me to Madam Tanith. If she had really cared, she would have come looking for me a lot sooner. While at home, I needed to gather more clothes and other essentials so I could stay at Anevae's for a while. The vampire couldn't enter the house unless he was invited, but that didn't make me feel any more comfortable leaving her alone.

About five minutes later, I walked up the steps to Anevae's front porch in fresh clothes, with a duffle bag slung over my shoulder and a bag of groceries in hand. As I knocked on the door, I surveyed the area for threats, but the vampire was long gone.

"Are you planning to stay for a while?" Anevae asked, chuckling as she opened the door.

"Maybe. Is that okay?" I asked, concern lacing my voice.

"Of course! I love having you around. Did you seriously bring some of your groceries with you?"

My face flushed with embarrassment when I realized how much I had actually brought with me. "I don't want things to go bad, and I also want to contribute since I'll clearly be eating here with you."

Sauntering inside, I headed to the kitchen. I placed everything on the counter and then put away all the groceries I had brought. Anevae scooped up my toiletries and clothes to take upstairs.

My stomach growled as I scoured the cabinets and fridge for lunch ideas. I found all the ingredients for grilled cheese and tomato soup, so I rounded them up, pulled down a pan, and got started.

When Anevae walked in, she took a big whiff and smiled. "How is it that you know so many of the things I love without even asking?"

Grinning, I responded, "I didn't know this was something you enjoyed. I guess I just have the intuition to know what you like. Help me out with this soup while I make the sandwiches. Please?" Looking over at her, I batted my eyelashes.

Giggling, she picked up the spoon to start stirring the soup. We stood there in silence for a few moments. I glanced at her every few seconds and admired how thoroughly she concentrated on her task. Her lips were pursed, and her eyebrows furrowed.

When she noticed I was staring, she furrowed her eyebrows further. "What?"

"You're adorable when you're concentrating," I whispered.

"You're supposed to be paying attention to our sandwiches. Don't let mine burn!"

Chuckling, I refocused on my task. After the last one was golden brown, I placed two sandwiches on each plate and retrieved bowls for the soup. Anevae took them from me and poured a ladle full in each bowl.

When everything was plated, we sat in silence and ate. After eating my last bit of food, I pushed my dishes forward slightly, then put my chin in my hand and watched Anevae.

"What would you like to do for the rest of the day?" I asked quietly.

"I'm not sure. I'd love to start more of my experiments in the greenhouse, but I don't have to now. I already wrote down the important stuff for the one I started outside, so I won't have to worry about that until I check everything in the next few days. What would you like to do?"

"I'll do anything as long as it means being with you. I'd just rather stay inside. I think we're going to get some rain later. The sky was looking a little dark when I got back," I lied.

"Well, come help me in the greenhouse, and then maybe we can come back inside and watch some more movies."

"Sounds like a plan. Let's clean up these dishes first."

# Chapter Nineteen

## Anevae

Maeyve and I watched movie after movie until we couldn't keep our eyes open anymore. We climbed into bed around 11 p.m., sleeping with our limbs tangled together as if we couldn't bear the thought of being separated. The next morning, I awoke wrapped up in her arms. Sighing, I snuggled in and closed my eyes, soaking up the moment. I felt safe, and it was refreshing.

After lying there for a few more minutes, I got up to use the bathroom. As I stood there, washing my hands and preparing to wash my face, Maeyve snuck up behind me and wrapped her hands around my waist.

Leaning down, she placed a kiss on my neck. "Good morning, beautiful," she whispered in my ear before nipping at the lobe.

Giggling, I wiped my hands dry and turned to plant a kiss on her lips. "Good morning, gorgeous. How did you sleep?"

"Sleeping next to you is a dream come true. I haven't slept this well in years. You might not be able to get rid of me now."

Grinning at her reflection in the mirror, I responded honestly, "I might enjoy that, actually."

Scoffing, she turned me to face her. "We'll have to see how much you actually enjoy me always bugging you. If you're not careful, you'll never finish any of your work."

Placing a hand on her chest, I smirked. "Lucky for you, plants take time to grow, so I have some free time on my hands."

"I can think of a few ways for us to use up some of that free time," she murmured before drawing her bottom lip into her mouth and biting down with one of her pronounced canines. Desire flooded my veins, and a throbbing began in my core.

"Now I'm intrigued. Why don't you show me? I think I have a little time to spare right now," I whispered, looking up at her through my lashes.

The next thing I knew, Maeyve had lifted me off my feet, positioning her hands perfectly under my ass. Instinctively, I wrapped my legs around her waist and my hands around her neck, tangling in her soft hair. Our lips collided as she turned back to the bedroom. I let out a soft moan as her hands gripped my ass tightly. With my lips slightly parted, she slipped her tongue into my mouth, exploring it.

When we reached the bed, she climbed onto it and laid me down gently, resting my head on the pillows. She trailed kisses across my jaw and down to my neck, stopping to bite me lightly. As she made her way down, her body grazed against my hardened nipples, and I grabbed onto her shoulders. When she reached my chest, she slid my camisole down to expose my breasts. Palming one, she licked at the nipple of the other. Soft moans escaped my lips as she began to move her tongue in slow circles around the stiff peak and piercing that adorned it. Looking up at me through her lashes, I could see the mischievous glint in her eyes. She lapped up the saliva that had collected on my nipple before sucking my hardened peak into her mouth and biting down. I let out a yelp followed by another moan as white spots dotted my vision. Slowly, her teeth grazed down my nipple until they reached the piercing, and she let go.

Raising onto her elbows again, she glanced down at my nipple. Quietly, she mumbled, "Oops. I'm sorry. Does that hurt?"

Panting from the desire coursing through my body, I replied, "Why are you sorry? That felt amazing."

I followed Maeyve's gaze to my breast, where there was blood pooling around my nipple. Not sure where it was coming from, I raised my hand to wipe away the blood. Maeyve grasped my hand and pulled it away before lowering her mouth back down to my breast.

She licked up the blood and moaned. As soon as her head lifted, I saw two faint scratches from her teeth. Surprised, I looked back up to Maeyve, meeting her gaze. Her eyes had darkened, and desire surged through my body. Her mouth returned to my breast, sucking my nipple into her mouth again. I let out a loud moan and gripped her shoulder tighter with my free hand.

Releasing my nipple with a pop, she sat up on her knees and trailed her eyes over my body. Humming, she ran her hands up the outsides of my thighs and gripped my shorts, pulling them off with my underwear. Then, she reached for my hand, urging me to sit up so she could pull off my camisole.

Glancing back into my eyes, she whispered, "You're so beautiful. I could tell you every moment of every day, and that still wouldn't be enough to express just how beautiful you are."

Blushing, I whispered, "You're too sweet."

"I only speak the truth."

Then, she claimed my mouth with hers and pushed me onto my back. We kissed for a few minutes before she wiggled down to position herself between my thighs. Just the sight of her being there had me dripping wet for her.

She stared up at me through her long lashes with a Cheshire grin spread across her face. "I can't wait to devour this sweet pussy."

The throbbing in my core intensified in anticipation. A sly grin spread across my face. "What are you waiting for?"

I didn't think it was possible, but her eyes darkened even further. Sliding her hands under my thighs, she lifted my hips and said, "You better watch that mouth of yours. It's going to get you in trouble at some point."

With a breathy laugh, I licked my lips. She turned her head and bit me roughly on the thigh. I gasped loudly. When she released my thigh from her mouth, she turned her head to lick up my wet slit right to my clit.

Letting out a long breath, I sighed. "Please keep going."

Tongue still lapping at my clit, she huffed out a laugh. Working one hand out from under my hip, she slid two fingers into me, pumping in and out. I threw my head back with a loud moan. Then, she sucked my clit into her mouth. Pleasure swirled throughout my body, and my walls tightened around her fingers. Maeyve's other hand tightly gripped my hip as a growl erupted from her chest.

That sound was something I'd never heard during sex, but, damn, was it intoxicating. Reaching a hand down, I grasped a handful of Maeyve's hair. With the other hand, I reached up and pinched my nipple. Panting, I could feel myself rising closer to my climax.

"Fuck, Maeyve. I'm not going to last much longer," I whimpered.

She began thrusting in deeper and harder with her fingers, skimming the sensitive spot up high. Arching my back, my moans grew louder. Maeyve released my clit, and before I could protest, she bit down.

I exploded, my orgasm hitting me as I screamed, "Maeyve! Oh my God. Maeyve! Fuck!"

Panting, I released her hair and my nipple. She continued until I stopped shaking.

Slipping her fingers from my wet folds, she slowly slid them into her mouth, one by one, licking up every last bit of my arousal that coated her hand while she held eye contact with me. "Mmm. You taste so sweet. I would devour this pussy for every meal: breakfast, lunch, dinner, all the snacks in between, and then dessert to end the day."

Climbing up my body, she bit my lip and slid her tongue into my mouth so I could taste myself. I wrapped my hands around her neck, pulling her deeper into the kiss. Arousal coiled through my body again, thinking of how her pussy tasted.

I wrapped my legs around her waist and flipped us over so I was straddling her. Grinding my hips against hers, she moaned into my mouth.

When I sat up, I whispered, "Your turn."

"Uh-oh. Should I be scared now?"

"Why would you be scared?"

Smirking, Maeyve met my gaze. "Hmm. I'm not sure. Have I been a bad girl? Do I deserve a punishment?"

I stopped what I was doing and sat up ramrod straight, staring at her with my eyes wide. At that moment, all I could think about was the punishments I had received from my ex-fiance. *Fuck. I can't be thinking about this right now. She is not him; she is* NOT *him!*

Maeyve's smile fell, and her brows furrowed. "What's wrong?"

I could feel my panic rising—my heart rate doubled, and my breathing grew ragged. *No, no, no, no, no. She is* NOT *him. It's okay. Get yourself together!*

Maeyve reached up, cupping my face to get me to focus on her. "Please talk to me. Everything is okay. What happened?"

Instinctively, I tried to remove her hands from my face, but she stayed steady, holding on.

"Hey, hey. Please talk to me. It's okay. Breathe," she said calmly.

But everything in my brain wasn't calm then; it was a whirlwind of panic. I was in fight-or-flight mode and needed to get off of her. When I shoved her chest, she let me go, and I ran into the bathroom, slamming the door.

# Chapter Twenty

## Maeyve

*What the fuck just happened?*

I flew off the bed and ran to the bathroom door. When I tried to open it, the knob didn't move—it was locked. I had to get in there to make sure she was okay.

"Anevae, please let me in."

On the other side of the door, all I could hear was Anevae's sobs. *Fuck. What happened? What did I say?*

"Anevae, baby, please?"

A few minutes later, she opened the door, wrapped in her white robe. Her eyes were bloodshot, her face streaked with tears, and my heart broke. I quickly pulled her to me, encasing her in my arms, and stroked her hair. She clung to me as she began crying again.

We stood there for several minutes before she took a deep breath and whispered, "I'm sorry."

Confused, I stepped back to look into her eyes. "You don't need to be sorry. There's clearly something bothering you, and I just want to help you through it. Did I say something? Do something?"

Looking back to the floor, she mumbled, "It's nothing."

Tipping her chin up, I said, "Please look at me. This is not nothing. You're upset about something... Does this have to do with your ex?"

Her eyes welled with tears as she nodded.

"How can I help you?" I asked quietly.

She gripped my wrist and said, "I think it's time I tell you about him. You won't understand unless I tell you the whole story."

"Please don't push yourself to tell me this story if it's going to be too hard on you."

Shaking her head, she squeezed my wrist. "I need to talk to you about it, especially if we want to continue this relationship for any length of time. I'm going to put my pajamas back on. Will you please go downstairs and make some coffee? We can sit at the island or on the couch; I don't really care right now."

My pulse quickened, but I tried to remain composed. *What would she have to tell me?* Giving her a quick kiss, I did as she asked and met her on the couch about ten minutes later.

After getting comfortable on the couch, she took her coffee from me and quickly thanked me. Holding the hot mug in her hands, she took a small sip.

When she met my gaze again, she began, "My senior year of high school was one of the best years I'd ever had. I was a straight-A student with a bright future ahead of me—I was accepted into Yale, one of the Ivy League universities. During that year, I met a guy named Ambrose, and we instantly fell in love. Being so naive, I thought he was the love of my life. He initially treated me like a princess, but Eiri tried to warn me about what she'd heard from other people at school. At the time, I brushed her off because she was my younger sister who didn't know a thing about love.

"At my graduation party that summer, Ambrose proposed to me. I was over the moon, and my parents were happy for me; they loved

Ambrose. Most of my friends were concerned about how fast things were moving in our relationship. Again, I ignored everyone because they didn't know us or how we felt about each other."

After sniffling several times, she sipped her coffee and continued, "About a month before school started back up, Ambrose and I moved into a rental home close to our respective universities. When we got settled, things began to change between us. We would argue over the smallest things—whose turn it was to do the dishes, what we'd eat for dinner and more. During these arguments, there were times he'd get so angry he put holes in the walls of our home.

"When school started, he began limiting my interactions with friends. At first, I wasn't allowed to spend time with my male friends. I didn't have many, and schoolwork was piling up, so it didn't bother me too much. Then, I couldn't go to parties without him. We were in college, and there were parties all the time. I wasn't popular by any means, but friends often invited me.

"This sparked a whole string of arguments between us. He told me that no matter what, he was the most important thing in my life, and I needed to treat him as such. One night, I tried to go to a movie with some friends, and he tracked me down. He claimed there was a family emergency, but once we got to the car, he smacked me across the face and told me that I 'needed to remember my place.' When we got home, I ran directly to our room and began crying. He rushed in behind me, apologizing profusely. He told me he 'didn't know why he did that' and he was 'so sorry' and he'd 'make it up to me.' I don't know why I didn't call my family then. Over the following days, he brought me gifts, begging me to forgive him. Like an idiot, I did. I thought it was a one-time thing and that it would never happen again. Our arguments stopped for a few months after that."

"I'm so sorry, Anevae," I said, reaching to grab her hand and let her know she was safe.

She stiffly accepted my consolation but whispered, "That wasn't even the worst of it."

My heart stopped. What she'd told me was bad enough as it was. If I ever came across the asshole, I'd give him the slow, torturous death he deserved.

Taking her hand back, she clutched onto her coffee mug again. "Our arguments resumed, and his anger grew with each one. I finally stopped going anywhere besides home, school, and occasionally the grocery store. I hoped that if I stopped going anywhere without him, our arguments would be better. It didn't; he just found new things to yell at me for.

"The first and only time I threatened to leave him, he beat me to the brink of unconsciousness. When he was done, he cried and held me as he said, 'You made me do this to you. You forced my hand.' After that, I became scared for my life and withdrew from everyone, including my family. I didn't want them to see me at this low point. I didn't want them to get in the middle; I was worried he'd kill them if they did."

A tear slid down her cheek, and I could understand the pain she felt because, once upon a time, I had felt something similar. Scooting closer, I put my hand on her leg but avoided crowding her space unless she wanted me there.

After taking a shaky breath, she continued, "When Eiri graduated high school, keeping her away became more difficult. She had been accepted into the same school as me, Yale, so she moved into an apartment down the street from the home I shared with Ambrose. To keep myself away from her, Ambrose helped me come up with reasons why I couldn't see her. We were successful for a while.

"One day, I ran into Eiri on my way home from school. When she saw me, she rushed to hug me, but then she noticed my bruised lip and the discoloration under my eye that I couldn't cover up with makeup. She pulled me off the sidewalk and interrogated me, asking what had happened to my face. I tried to play it off as a fall, but she wasn't falling for it. In reality, Ambrose had beat me again over not doing the dishes a few nights prior. Eiri saw right through my bullshit and knew Ambrose had hurt me. I tried to cover up for him, but she wasn't having it, so I took off. I was running late and already knew Ambrose would be mad when I got home.

"The moment I walked through our front door, he was on me, yelling and demanding to know where I was. But he didn't let me speak before yanking me back to our room by the hair. Once we were in there, he tried to ask the same questions, and when I didn't answer fast enough, he grabbed me by the throat, bringing me to his level. I couldn't breathe, and I was clawing at his hand so he'd let me go, but when he did, I rolled my ankle. Displays of weakness angered him, so when I whimpered, he told me to 'shut up, or I'll give you something to cry about.'"

More tears welled in her eyes. I reached up to wipe one away as it started falling down her cheek. "You're safe now," I whispered.

She shook her head vigorously, ripping her face away from my hand. "I'm not done. There's still a little more to this story... When Ambrose stormed out of our room, I heard a knock on the front door. Ambrose answered it to find my dad and sister on the other side. Eiri knew something was wrong, and I needed help, so she got our dad to save me. That was the last time I saw Ambrose. My family took me home that weekend, and I didn't return to school for a few weeks. I moved in with Eiri when I went back. It took me *months* to be able to be alone because I never knew if he was coming back. I haven't been in a long-term relationship since. I've hooked up with some men but didn't want to let anyone else in. You're the first person I've told about this besides my family and therapist."

Staring down at the empty mug in her hands, she let her tears fall. I took it from her and placed it on the coffee table beside mine. When I turned back to her, I pulled her into my lap and let her cry. I stroked her hair with one hand and rubbed her back with the other. I would protect her with my life if that meant she was safe; I would never let another person cause her harm again.

# Chapter Twenty-One

## *Anevae*

Maeyve and I spent the rest of that day relaxing. It was rough to tell her about Ambrose, but she deserved to know. She comforted me and made me feel safe, seen, and important. I wasn't sure what to think of our "relationship," but I didn't care. I didn't need her to love me; I just wanted her around.

The next morning, I woke up wrapped in Maeyve's arms again. I wanted to wake up like that every day for the rest of my life. I snuggled in for a bit longer before finally getting up to start the day.

During breakfast, we discussed our plans for the day.

"I know there won't be much, if any, change in my plants, but I need to check on them today," I said.

Maeyve jutted out her bottom lip, pouting. "Do we have to? I don't want to go outside. I think it's supposed to be chilly out today. I want to cuddle up on the couch again. Maybe you could read me a book today? We can change things up."

"We can do that *after* we go check on my experiments. It's not going to take long! Maybe ten minutes *tops*. If you don't want to go with me, stay here, but I need to do this for my work."

"*Fine.* I guess we'll go. But if it's cold out there, you owe me," she grumbled.

"It's almost summer! It's not going to be cold. Let's go get dressed."

After getting dressed, we went into the greenhouse and tended to the plants there. Once that was done, we made our way outside. Maeyve slid her hand into mine when we walked out the door, and I smiled at her. She gave my hand a comforting squeeze and grinned back at me.

As we reached the garden plot, Maeyve became agitated, her eyes darting around like she was searching for something. I tried to act like I didn't notice. She squeezed my hand and pulled me to her. "I think I heard something out in the woods. I want to go check it out. I'll be right back, okay? Do NOT go anywhere else. Please."

"Okay. I'm just going to check on these plants and make some notes. Be careful."

Before she left, she planted a quick kiss on my lips and another on my temple. Then, I watched her walk away into the woods. When she was just out of sight, I turned to my garden.

I was working for about five minutes when I felt a presence behind me. Thinking it was Maeyve, I kept working. Then, a pair of arms wrap tightly around my midsection. Dread coiled in the pit of my stomach. My gaze drifted down to the tanned, hairy arms that were wrapped around my center, arms that most certainly did not belong to Maeyve. I began screaming as loud as I could and thrashing in the stranger's arms. When that got me nowhere, I threw my head back, aiming for his face. The only thing that did was make him angry.

After several long seconds, the black fox appeared from inside the woods. As it stalked toward us, it bared its teeth and snarled. *What is the fox doing here? Where's Maeyve?* The stranger's deep laugh startled me. He continued backing up with me, still wrapped in his arms.

134

"You think you scare me, little fox?" The stranger asked in a husky voice. "Quit acting like you can protect her somehow. You're just a worthless being that should've been disposed of long ago. On the other hand, she was meant for greatness, and His Majesty is growing tired of waiting for her. Now, if you'll excuse us," the stranger said, his voice taunting.

The fox's orange eyes met mine. When a stray tear fell down my cheek, the fox crept forward, still baring its teeth and snarling.

The man laughed. "You don't scare me one fucking bit, Maeyve. You're nothing but a filthy whore, and you always will be. Royalty like her will never mix with scum like you. His Majesty would never allow it. Even if she is impure. Fucking Cordilaen, choosing that disgusting wolf over her duties. But this one will honor her responsibilities to the crown. I'll see to it myself."

As the last words left the stranger's lips, the fox leaped and latched onto one of the stranger's arms. He hissed in pain and loosened his grip on me. I fell to the ground and quickly scrambled to my feet.

Out of curiosity and pure stupidity, I turned to look at my attempted abductor. His back was to me, but he was a tall, muscular man with hair black as night, slicked back and cut in a similar fashion to how my dad wore his.

Flailing his arm, he began flinging the fox around to get it off. I wasn't sure how he was doing it because the fox was huge and likely weighed at least a hundred and fifty pounds. Eyes focusing on the fox, I remembered what he'd called it—Maeyve.

I knew I had to help the fox, especially if it was Maeyve. I could think about what had happened later. Taking off toward the cabin, I flung the greenhouse door open. Hurrying inside, I searched for anything I could use as a weapon against the man.

The best thing I could find was a shovel. *Welp, this is going to have to work for now.*

Just as soon as I was about to run back out the door, I heard a loud yelp. Clutching to the shovel, I took a step outside. The fox was lying on the ground next to one of the garden plots.

I ran as fast as I could, not caring if the man captured me. If the fox was Maeyve, I needed to make sure she was safe.

I slid up to the fox, placing a hand on its side to see if it was breathing. The fox yelped, and I pulled my hand back. *Was it hurt? What happened? Was it okay?*

Knowing the fox was alive, I scanned my surroundings for the man. When I didn't see him, I glanced back at the fox. I couldn't lift it alone, but I didn't want to leave it by itself outside; moving it would hurt it, and I didn't want that either. Reluctantly, I retreated to the cabin. I could watch it from the window to make sure it got up. If it didn't, I'd have to worry about that later.

Once I was inside, I stood at the kitchen counter. As I glanced out the window, the gravity of everything hit me. Could I have been dreaming? Pinching myself, I determined it was, in fact, *not* a dream. Terror crept up, and I began to question everything I knew. With my mind swirling nonstop, I shook violently, and my head spun. An intense wave of nausea hit me, and I rushed to the bathroom.

After several minutes, my stomach had completely emptied itself and finally settled. I sat with my back to the wall and cried. *Who was that man? How did he know my mom's name? Why was 'His Majesty' looking for me? Who was he?*

As I sat there, question after question whirled through my mind, but then my thoughts drifted back to the fox. *Could the fox really have been Maeyve?* Every shred of logic left intact said she couldn't have been the fox, but then my mom's stories about Caellaias crept into my mind. *Could it really be?*

When I got up to check on the fox, it wasn't lying in the grass anymore. I hoped it was okay... I hoped Maeyve was okay. Tears rolled down my cheeks as I slid to the floor. Burying my face in my hands, I drew my knees up to my chest.

# Chapter Twenty-Two

## Maeyve

Latching onto the vampire's arm, his sour blood coated my tongue. But I didn't care. Anevae dropped to the ground as his grip loosened. He began thrashing me around, and I clenched my jaw around his arm even tighter. The bastard wouldn't take her. I wouldn't let that happen. I didn't give a fuck who he thought he was or who he thought Anevae was; she was not his. She may not be mine, but I would protect her like she was.

The sound of the greenhouse door creaking open reached my ears. Anevae was safe, a small amount of solace that allowed me to relax. The vampire took advantage of my distraction and smacked my body against a nearby tree. I felt one of my ribs crack. Releasing my jaw, I yelped in pain and slumped to the ground.

The vampire hissed, "I should kill you where you lay, but I've been given strict orders not to harm you. We'll see each other again soon enough."

As the vampire's footsteps retreated, I tried to roll onto my back, but a searing pain spread through my side. Letting out another, quieter yelp, I gave up, coming to rest on my unaffected side, and cursed to myself.

Sucking in deep breaths, I tried to relax, and the bone began to heal. I didn't hear Anevae come up behind me. *What the fuck is she doing out here? I don't even know if the vampire went back to Caellaias. He could still be around, waiting to take her when I'm not capable of protecting her. Fuck.*

Then, she knelt behind me and touched my side. I let out another yelp, and she jerked her hand away. I wished I could tell her I was okay and that she needed to get back into the house before the vampire came back. I wouldn't be able to live with myself if something happened to her.

After a few minutes, she stood back up, and the grass rustling beneath her feet grew further away. When I heard the greenhouse door slam shut, I breathed a sigh of relief. I was thankful she went inside. Once I was healed enough, I'd find my clothes and make sure she was okay. If I moved too much during the healing process, it would stall, or the bone wouldn't heal properly. *She's safe. She's inside. The vampire is gone.* Those were the words I chanted in my head until I could finally move.

As the pain eased, I sprung to my feet with a wince and rushed toward my clothes, waiting to shift until I reached them. When I began shifting, the pain and healing in my rib made things ten times harder. I had to stop several times, so I didn't pass out.

After getting dressed, I limped to the cabin's front door. Standing on the porch, I listened for Anevae; she was crying, likely scared for her life.

Raising my hand, I pounded on the door.

# Chapter Twenty-Three

## *Anevae*

I wasn't sure how long I'd been crying when I heard a loud pounding at the front door. The sound startled me, but I rushed to peek out the window. I was confident that if it were the unfamiliar man, he wouldn't be knocking on my door. But with what had just happened, I wanted to be sure of who it was. Outside, pounding on the door again, was Maeyve. She had blood smeared across her face and was visibly favoring one leg over the other. Her shirt was torn in spots, and her hair was a mess. I hurried to the door and fumbled with the locks to let her in.

A wave of relief washed over me as I ran to the door and pulled her inside. "Oh, thank God you're okay."

After guiding her to the couch, I rushed to grab first aid supplies and washcloths to clean her up. When I returned to the living room, she was pacing.

"What are you doing? You're hurt! Please sit," I requested.

She turned to me, eyes a fluorescent orange, and murmured, "Anevae, we need to talk about what happened outside."

When I focused on her eyes, I remembered the fox staring at me as the man held me. She was the fox, and she saved my life. Rushing over to her, I urged her to sit. I had to make sure she was okay and clean her up. Sitting down next to her, I began to wipe away the blood from her face.

Still looking at the floor, she asked, "What are your parents' names?"

My hand froze. "The man mentioned my mom. Her name is Cordilaen. My dad's name is Roarc."

She closed her eyes and cursed, "Shit. This is bad, but things are starting to make so much more sense. What have your parents told you about themselves?"

Her question confused me. "My parents never talked about where they came from, and I knew very little about their lives before I was born. Things may make sense to you, but they don't make any sense to me right now. Why don't you just tell me what you have to tell me? I need you to explain to me what's going on."

"I'm very sorry you're hearing this from me. Your parents should have been honest with you. But they had their chance..." she trailed off before sucking in a deep breath and blurting out, "The man out there wasn't really a man at all; he was a vampire. From what it sounds like, the king has sent him here to retrieve you –"

I could feel my eyes double in size. "What king? The king of where? Why would he want me? Is my mom royalty of some sort?" My mind ran a million miles a second.

She placed her hand on my face and brought my eyes back to hers. "Your mom, Cordilaen, is a faerie princess who has been missing for decades, and your dad, Roarc, is the shifter lord's second son. We all come from another realm that is interconnected with this one called Caellaias."

As soon as she mentioned Caellaias, I gasped and shoved at her. "No. No. No. That's not true. That can't be true. Caellaias is just a place my mom made up to entertain my sister and me."

Her voice was soft as she took my hand. "I assure you that Caellaias is real. It's not something your mom just made up. I'm not sure why your parents didn't tell you about who they are. No one ever knew where Cordilaen went or who she went with, but everyone knew she had glamour magic, making the efforts to locate her that much more difficult. Roarc disappeared around the same time that Cordilaen did, but his disappearance wasn't as concerning because he wasn't as important to the king. I'm sure no one thought they'd left together."

While I sat there, trying to process everything, Maeyve got up and began pacing. Suddenly, she stopped in front of me and said, "That explains why there *was* a ward around your cabin. There's a portal to Caellaias in these woods. Your parents likely wanted to protect you, but why the hell wouldn't they tell you about Caellaias with you being so close?"

"There was a what? A ward? What is that?"

"A ward is a type of spell that protects an area, acting like a barrier between your home and the rest of the world. As long as you were inside, no magical being could cross it until they were invited. Could you not sense it? Did you even realize when it was destroyed?"

"No, I had no clue anything was out there; until a few minutes ago, I didn't even think Caellaias was real. When was it destroyed?"

"It happened the night before I came pounding on your door frantically. Do you remember anything about that night?"

"I watched movies with Eiri until really late, then she went home, and I went upstairs to bed."

"Was anything odd to you that night?"

"Well, I was really tired, like more so than normal. But it was the first day I hadn't done much, so I attributed it to that."

"Hmmm. That's weird," she said, then started pacing again. Coming to another stop, she met my gaze. "I wonder why I still can't sense your magic. There's no way you're powerless with your parents' lineages."

"You said my mom has glamour magic, right? Could she have covered things up with that? I have no clue how all of this works."

"That's definitely how she hid you all for so long, but that wouldn't be the reason I can't sense it now. I wonder if she's been giving you a suppressant?"

"How would I know? This is just so much to process."

Maeyve came to kneel before me. Grabbing my hand, she said, "You likely wouldn't know. As long as I'm around, I won't let anything happen to you. I'm sorry you haven't been told about the world your parents come from."

"I know more than you think. My mom used to tell my sister and me stories about Caellaias and all of the beings from there. Maybe she knew she couldn't protect me forever. My dad always told me that Caellaias and everything my mom told me wasn't real. Why? Why not prepare Eiri and me? Why get mad at my mom when she was just trying to educate us? Did he think he could protect us forever? I'm sorry. I have so many questions."

Maeyve sighed as she looked at our hands. "I know this is a lot. I wish I could answer every question you have, but I don't know what their intentions were for keeping things from you girls. That's a question for them."

Gasping, I remembered one of my mom's stories. "Oh my God. My mom was Princess Laeney—Laeney is short for Cordilaen. My dad is the shifter lord's son. I know why they ran away! My grandfather tried to force my mom to marry a wealthy faerie, and she didn't want to. She never told us how they ran away. Shit. Then that means the king is my grandfather. But why did he send a vampire to bring me back to him? Why does he want me at all? Is he trying to lure my mother home? Or does he have ulterior motives?"

When Maeyve looked up at me, I didn't meet her gaze. We sat there in silence for several minutes until she whispered, "Anevae?"

Sliding my hand from hers, I finally looked at her again. "This can't be real. I have to be dreaming. I'm just an ordinary, boring woman; there's no such thing as Caellaias; my mom isn't a faerie, and my dad isn't a shifter; I'm not royalty. This is just a dream." Then I began shaking as other realizations hit me. "My lover isn't also a fox... shifter? And a vampire isn't trying to capture me to take me to my grandfather..." Burying my face in my hands, I began hyperventilating.

Maeyve climbed up on the couch next to me and pulled me onto her lap, encasing me in her arms. I hadn't had a panic attack in many years, but this was all too much information at once. My mind kept swirling as I tried to wrap my head around everything. Tears welled in my eyes, and I tried to wipe them away without success.

After a few moments, I unraveled myself from her arms, wiped my tears, took a few deep breaths, and looked at her. "I know why you got concerned when I mentioned the black fox now. It was you. Were you watching me before we met?" I asked, concern lacing my voice.

She dropped her eyes to the floor and nodded. "Yes, the fox you've been seeing is my fox form. I was curious about you and the ward surrounding your house. My intrigue intensified when you visited my house, and I checked on you more often. I haven't wanted to take my eyes off you since then."

"If it'll help me come to terms with all of this, will you do something for me?" I lifted my gaze to Maeyve, who stood silently, waiting. "Will you...show me? Your transformation, I mean?"

After taking a deep breath, she said, "If that's what you need, I'll happily do it."

She took a few steps back and then began stripping off her clothes. As she removed each layer, my eyes skimmed over her body, drinking her in. When she started to transform into her fox form, I was awestruck. Fur began sprouting all over her body, black and orange, just like her hair. The shape of her face changed, and the bones in her extremities broke, repositioning themselves; it looked painful. But just as fast as it had started, the transformation was complete. In front of me was the black fox I'd seen numerous times over the last few days.

Once she was fully shifted, she looked up at me with her beautiful orange eyes. I stood to approach her without thinking, but her ears flattened, and she whimpered.

"I'm sorry. I just want to get a closer look at you. This is all new to me, and I want to know everything. If you don't want me to get close, I will stay right here, but I won't hurt you," I said as I knelt on the floor.

Maeyve's eyes locked onto mine through thick black fur. Hesitantly, she slunk forward and sat directly in front of me. She was larger than the other foxes I had encountered in the past; her head was still easily as large as mine, and her paws were still about the same size as my hands. Her shoulders were up to my hip when she stood on all fours. Her black and orange fur looked soft and fluffy. I wanted nothing more than to run my fingers through it.

I raised my hand as a request to stroke her fur if she'd allow it. She bent her head toward me and bumped my hand with her wet nose. When I didn't move my hand, she licked it. The sandpaper-like texture of her tongue made me snatch my hand back. I didn't expect her tongue to have such a rough texture.

She whimpered and lay down with her head on her paws. I slowly reached out to pet her soft head and ears and gave her a small, sad smile. I couldn't believe it was all real.

We stayed silent as I stroked her fur, and after a few minutes, I sighed with regret. "We need to talk some more. Can you please change back into your human form and get dressed?"

Maeyve got up, licked my face, and stepped back over to her clothes, where she returned to her human form. The transformation was so fast I might have missed it if I were to blink. She put her clothes back on and pulled me onto the couch. When she sat beside me, she was ready to listen.

We sat silently for several moments before I began, "I don't even know where to start. I'm worried that if I confront my parents, they'll never let me out of their sight again. Or they'll find a way to force me back home. Fuck. What if the vampire is going after Eiri, too?

Why does the king want *me?*" All the questions continuously circling through my head had my pulse quickening, and my breathing grew ragged.

Maeyve grasped my hand, and a jolt went through my body that was different from the one I usually felt when she touched me.

Ripping my hand from her grasp, I asked, "What the fuck was that? That is *not* like the normal tingling sensation I get when we touch."

She let out a nervous laugh before she spoke. "That was me. We're not going to get anywhere with you panicking, and one of the many benefits of being a succubus is my calming ability. Please take a deep breath. Let's tackle one thing at a time."

"Wait a minute, did you say you're part succubus? Like 'luring people in and attracting them' part succubus? Oh my god. Is that why I've been so attracted to you?!" My voice raised an octave with every question spewing from my mouth. Now, not only was I confused, but I was furious. "You made me like you, didn't you? You attracted me and used me, didn't you?!"

Maeyve's jaw dropped at my accusations. Her eyes darkened with anger as she lowered her voice and grasped my chin, "You listen to me right now. Luring people is an ability that succubi have, and yes, some use it for evil. I can't help what I am, but I *can* control my abilities. I have *never* once lured you to me since we met, and I would *never* do that to you. This connection between us has been genuine. I've felt the same pull you have since we met. Do not come at me with the human myths of my kind again. I'm sure you know nothing about what a true succubus is."

The anger in her voice put me on the defensive, and I felt angry right back, but her grip on my chin was comforting. Whenever our skin touched, it felt like the world was right, and I didn't want to leave her. I was conflicted about whether to pull back from her or lean in closer. Something about her anger turned me on, which only irritated me. What if she was using this to convince me to stay? She sent the jolt only moments ago to calm me down. Finally, my brain took over, and I ripped my chin out of her grasp.

Once free, I pushed back and rose from the couch, wanting to be anywhere but there having that conversation. I didn't know what to believe besides what I had seen. I knew she was indeed a fox shifter, but I knew nothing about her succubus powers or what they could do. I needed to process everything; I could only think of doing that if she wasn't in the house with me.

"I want you to leave. I *need* you to leave. I can't do this right now. I can't even think straight when you're around. This is all too much, and I don't even know how I feel right now."

Panic took over Maeyve's face as she scrambled to her feet and attempted to grab my hand. I shuffled backward to stay out of her grasp. Then, the anger returned.

She stopped and screamed, "Fine! You want me to leave you alone?! I've done *nothing* but try to please you these last few days. I've put myself at risk for you numerous times now, and I haven't even expected any appreciation! I just wanted to explain things to you. I wanted you to understand. I showed you my fox, which I have *never* done for *anyone* before! I've never trusted anyone the way I trust you. I've never *felt* this way about anyone before, but you want me to leave? *Fine.* Good luck figuring things out with the vampire stalking your home. You don't know anything about our world." When she finished, she marched around the house, grabbing some of her things before she stomped out the front door.

For a moment, I just stood there, staring at the door. Then, the weight of what I had just done settled over me. I scrambled to the door and threw it open, but Maeyve was already gone, her things scattered on the ground. As I stood there, my mind began to race, and panic took over.

My heart pounded a million miles a minute, and my breaths became more rapid and shallow. Everything she said as she left had come at me full force. I had no clue how I would handle the vampire, and I didn't want to include my parents unless I had to. They'd kept enough about Caellaias from me, and I didn't want them fighting my battles anymore.

Slamming the door shut, I placed my back to it and willed my fear to ease, but the more I thought about going outside, even just to get away from the property and the vampire, I began to shake and feel lightheaded. *Fuck. There's so much to process. I just need a minute.*

As I slid down the door, I closed my eyes, covered my ears, and screamed at the top of my lungs, letting loose all of the pain, fear, and anger until my throat was raw. When I couldn't scream anymore, I went back to the couch. I'd figure everything out at some point, but at that moment, I needed my sister.

Just as I sat down, a text came in.



*Perfect, but strange timing,* I thought to myself.

Zoning out for a few minutes, I weighed my options. I could tell her everything and have her think I was insane, or I could lie and try to handle all of this on my own. Whatever my decision, I needed to make it before Eiri got too concerned.

Pulling up her thread, I decided to lay out the truth.



Once I hit send, I started crying. I was scared and didn't know what to do. I also didn't want my sister to think I was crazy.

After sending the text, I wandered to the kitchen to get some water. My stomach was ready to empty itself again, but my mouth and throat were dry from the screaming I had done. I poured myself a glass and took a few sips. When I was done, I set it down on the island and sat at one of the barstools to wait for my sister.

# Chapter Twenty-Four

## Maeyve

I slammed the door behind me as I left Anevae's cabin. I'd felt like I was leaving a piece of me with her, but I tried to ignore it. Her words hurt me, and I couldn't entirely blame her for being mad. I was just trying to protect her in my own way. I shouldn't have kept things from her, but I was still trying to figure things out before dragging her into something she wasn't prepared for. *Damn, vampire.* At least I knew what and who she was now.

As I walked away, the cruelty of my words began to sink in, and a pit of regret formed in my gut. I spoke out of anger, wanting to hurt her as much as she had hurt me. When tears began welling in my eyes, I dropped everything I'd been carrying and shifted into my fox form to get home faster. With my injuries fully healed, the shift was painless.

I took off in a sprint, heading to my cabin. Behind me, I heard the door to Anevae's cabin open, but I wasn't turning around. She needed space? Fine. I'd give it to her. It didn't mean I wouldn't watch over her.

After the door slammed shut, I heard her scream. Panic filled me, and I stopped in my tracks. I wanted nothing more than to turn around to make sure she was okay, but I reminded myself that she wanted me to leave. I continued as my heart pounded and concern sank deep into my chest. I reassured myself that the vampire couldn't get inside her house without an invitation from Anevae.

When I reached my cabin, I shifted back into my human form and shoved the door open. I was still angry and concerned about Anevae, but depression began to settle in; I was alone again. Anevae made me feel alive and happy, unlike I'd ever felt before. For the first time in my life, it felt like someone actually cared about me. Tears welled in my eyes, and I wiped them away as I wandered into the bathroom.

I headed straight for the shower, making the water as hot as my skin would handle. Then, I stepped in, trying to melt away my disappointment and sadness. Whenever the water started to get cold, I'd turn the temperature up until it couldn't go up anymore. After exhausting the hot water, I forced myself to wash up and climb out of the shower.

Grabbing a towel from the rack, I wrapped myself up and plodded to my bedroom, where I collapsed onto my bed. I lay there staring at the ceiling, unsure what to do with myself. Unknowingly, I had started letting my life revolve around Anevae. She was something new and exciting, and after so many years of monotony, I welcomed the distraction and desire without a second thought. *How could I have been so careless?*

Arturo had been the closest thing to a friend I'd had in years. Since I avoided the towns as much as possible, I didn't interact with others. Until Anevae came along, I didn't think I needed friends; I didn't think I'd need anyone. I thought I'd be okay all alone, but she made me realize I was wrong. I was desperate to have her be a part of my life. I didn't know how much time she needed, but I knew I needed to tell her how I felt and explain what I could. I'd give her all the time in the world if it meant I could be with her.

Closing my eyes, I felt tears stream down my cheeks. I hated crying, but I gave in, rolled onto my side, and curled up into a ball, letting the tears flow. I'd check on her in a little bit, but for the time being, she was safe as long as she stayed inside her cabin.

# Chapter Twenty-Five

## Anevae

As I tried to clear my mind, I stared at my glass of water until I heard a knock at the front door. Nearly falling out of my chair, I regained my composure. Chances were it was my sister. Still, I crept to the window to confirm. Sure enough, she stood there wearing a garlic necklace, just as she had joked about in her text. I rushed to the door and threw it open. Reaching out, I yanked her inside and slammed the door shut, locking the deadbolt and slide lock I hadn't used since I moved in.

"Thank goodness you're here. I was so worried the vampire would get you," I said.

Eiri reached out and held me for a while as I gripped her tightly, never wanting to let her go. She grounded me at that moment. Out of everyone, my sister understood me the most; she'd been through everything with me. While I worried I may have sounded crazy, we grew up listening to our mom's stories about Caellaias and the beings that inhabited the kingdom.

Finally, Eiri shuffled me over to the couch. When I was settled, she retreated to the kitchen to make some tea. Our mom always did this when we were upset or not feeling well, and my sister and I kept the tradition.

When she returned, she sat and handed me my tea before calmly saying, "Start from the beginning."

We spent the rest of the day discussing what happened over the previous week; I divulged information that I wouldn't have told anyone else about the relationship I developed with Maeyve, what I learned about her, and how that affected me. Then, I told her what had happened with the vampire earlier in the day and how Maeyve had saved me. I explained that Maeyve was actually the black fox I had been seeing in the area. She stopped me multiple times to ask questions, making sure that I could trust what Maeyve had told me, but when I explained Maeyve's transformation into her fox form, Eiri finally understood.

"As concerned and suspicious as I am, I will always believe what you tell me. I would say that I think we should talk to Momma about this encounter you had with the vampire, but then she'll feel obligated to tell Poppa. We wouldn't be in this situation if they had prepared us in the first place. They've kept so much from us, and I don't feel like I can trust them anymore," Eiri said.

"Exactly. I'm just so angry at them! I don't want to be brought home and never be told I can leave again. I don't want them to fight our battles anymore. I'm sure there's a reason they never told us, but I don't understand why," I said.

Eiri nodded in agreement. "They need to realize and remember that we are grown women; we can make our own decisions, and if that means we don't want to go home, then we shouldn't have to. I wish they would have told us about Caellaias."

"I wish Momma could help and explain things without involving Poppa. She's always been the level-headed one. No wonder Poppa was always so defensive when Momma told us stories about Caellaias; who knows what else he's hiding from us? If we go home, who's to say they won't continue to keep things from us even though we deserve the truth?"

Eiri thought about it and agreed. "We will get this figured out. We need to do some investigating outside at some point, though."

As I looked at Eiri and processed what she said, terror took over, and I began to hyperventilate. What if the vampire was still out there, waiting for me? What if he took Eiri? There was no way that Eiri and I would be prepared to fend off a vampire. It was stupid to make Maeyve leave the way I did, but I needed space to breathe and my sister to talk things through with me. She was the only one who could understand why I was so upset. I'd have to reach out to her the next day so we could talk about things.

Eiri attempted to comfort me again. "Shh. Shh. One step at a time. We can do this."

She'd helped me through numerous panic attacks in the past, so we knew the best ways to calm them together. We used every technique we had developed over the years, but each one only seemed to help for a few minutes at a time.

When nothing was helping, I got up and began pacing until I got dizzy. Then I stopped and sat on the floor, pulling my knees as close to my chest as possible. Eiri joined me and rubbed my back to help ground me while I tried to talk myself out of my spiral.

"We'll work on getting out of this cabin one day at a time, but I cannot constantly bring you things, and I don't think things can be delivered here. It's worth a shot, but I highly doubt it will work," Eiri said quietly.

I was grateful to have her as my sister; she would do anything for me. But she deserved to live a life where she wasn't constantly caring for or worrying about me. Tears welled in my eyes. *I have to do something to fix this.*

"Let's do something to distract you for now. How about some movies or TV shows? We could watch some comedies to get you laughing," Eiri suggested.

I nodded. Eiri stood and headed to the kitchen to get some comfort foods while I found something to watch. I queued up a comedy I'd wanted to see, then went to the bathroom to splash some cold water on my face.

My reflection stared back at me; I looked awful. My long, crimson hair was a tangled mess. My eyes were bloodshot, and the skin around my eyes, cheeks, and nose was bright cherry red. Turning on the faucet, I collected some water and rubbed it onto my warm face.

When I was done, I returned to the living area, where Eiri waited. She had pulled some of my blankets out of their cubby and brought some pillows from my bed, which she arranged to allow for maximum comfort. I knew she hadn't planned to spend the night with me, but I also knew she'd do anything for me. She was more than happy to oblige if that meant an unexpected sleepover.

We watched a few movies, and halfway into the third, Eiri fell fast asleep. I quietly snuck off the couch to get some water and stretch. I was still overly tense but had calmed down some. I peered out the window as I stood at the sink to get my water. Just inside the tree line, the black fox was lying down on the floor of the woods, staring directly at me. Knowing Maeyve was still looking over me was comforting.

After drinking my water, I returned to the couch where my sister still slept. I turned the TV off, covered her with a blanket, and grabbed my pillow to take upstairs. Eiri didn't stir once.

I quietly climbed the stairs so I didn't wake her, heading for the bathroom to shower and prepare for bed. The shower felt amazing, with the hot water running over my sore body. Once I was dried off, I put on some pajamas, did my bedtime routine, and crawled into bed. I lay there awake for a while, tossing and turning. I still couldn't get my mind clear. Once I was comfortable enough, I drifted off to sleep.

# Chapter Twenty-Six

## *Anevae*

The following day, I awoke to Eiri lying in bed with me. She was playing on her phone, waiting for me to wake up. As I stirred, she looked over at me and smiled.

"How are you feeling this morning? Any better? How did you sleep?"

Rolling onto my back, I stretched. "Too many questions at once, Eiri."

"Well?" Eiri asked, pushing me for an answer.

"I slept alright. I dreamed about Caellaias, or at least the version I made from Momma's stories. I feel okay, though. I want to talk to Maeyve later."

Eiri dropped her phone on her chest and stared at me. "Vay, do you really think that's a good idea?"

Sitting up, I pulled my knees as close to my chest as possible. As I looked over at Eiri, I sighed. I was still nervous about opening back up to Maeyve, but she could help me, and I didn't want to get my parents involved. I felt betrayed by them.

"What other choice do I have?" I inquired. "We've already established that I don't want to involve our parents. Where else are we going to get information?"

A while later, we sat silently eating our breakfast, unsure what to say to the other. Eiri was persistent about exploring the grounds, but I couldn't bear the thought of going outside.

When Eiri finished her breakfast, she put her plate in the sink and said, "I think I should head out. I have an interview this afternoon but don't hesitate to call me if you need me. And please let me know how your discussion with Maeyve goes."

"Okay. Thank you."

"I'll call you after my interview. Love you."

"Sounds good. Love you too," I said and gave her a hug.

She stepped outside, and I watched her walk to her car. Once she was safely inside, I locked the door before heading to the greenhouse. I didn't want to go outside, so I would have to document my outdoor experiments from inside.

While I was checking my indoor experiments, there was a quiet knock on the greenhouse door. I jumped when I heard the sound, and my heart began pounding. I spun around to find Maeyve standing on the other side of the exterior door.

I walked across the greenhouse and cracked the door. "Hi. I'm actually kind of glad you're here."

"I need to explain some things to you," Maeyve said calmly.

"Okay. Come inside," I said as I stepped aside to let her in. If she had wanted to hurt me, she would have done so by now. Once she shuffled past me, I snapped the door shut, not wanting to let anyone or anything else in.

"I promise, no one is out there. I've been scouting the perimeter all morning. I needed to make sure you were safe. I can't bear the thought of something happening to you. Hell, I can't even handle being away from you anymore," Maeyve confessed.

"Thank you."

Maeyve sighed and looked at me. "Please understand that I had no idea who or what you were when you moved here. I'd like to tell you about my life before I came to this realm. Can we please sit for this? It's going to be a very long story."

Nodding, I motioned for her to go into the living room, where we sat opposite each other on the couch.

With a deep breath, she began her story. "My time in Caellaias was rough. My mother was a fox shifter who one day met an incubus. He tried to use his abilities to seduce her, but she was somehow able to deny him. That angered him, and he raped her. As a result, she ended up pregnant with me. Her family shunned her for having a baby out of wedlock, regardless of the circumstances surrounding my conception.

"Homeless, pregnant, and on the streets of western Maiviraea, she began working in a brothel to make ends meet. She found a new family there with the other girls, but my mother was an outcast thanks to her job. We didn't have a lot of money, so I received the bare minimum with my schooling. Being half-blooded and the daughter of a prostitute, people constantly looked down on me.

"Around the time I reached puberty, my mom wasn't making enough money to support us anymore. So the madam, Madam Tanith, forced her to pull me out of school, and she put me to work doing odd jobs to earn my keep. A couple of my old classmates were kind enough to bring me some of the study materials as they continued their education. I worked on that in my downtime to keep me busy. But if Madam Tanith caught me, I was lashed. There was nothing I could do to hide from her. She had eyes and ears everywhere." Maeyve shifted uncomfortably in her seat and began twirling her hair around her finger.

Sadness filled me. I couldn't keep myself from reaching out and grabbing her hand to show my support and ground her. My own trauma made me acutely aware of how talking about it could transport you back to that place. I'd experienced it every time I thought about Ambrose.

A tear rolled down her cheek as she looked down at our hands. "When I began to mature into a young woman, Madam Tanith ordered the other succubus in our brothel to teach me how to use my abilities. It didn't take long before I became proficient in my succubus skills, but with more practice, I learned I could use it for other purposes, like calming people.

"By the time I was thirteen, I had already seen my first client. The other succubus found out about my calming abilities during one of our training sessions, and she reported it back to Madam Tanith, who demanded to see me right away. She had developed a scheme that involved me using my abilities to lure powerful clients to her establishment. Night after night, I went out and convinced higher and higher-profile clients to come back to the brothel with me. I never found out what she did to them once I got them there. That guilt followed me for years.

"But I continued doing it because I was told these contracts would lead me toward freedom. It was all lies, of course. Lecherous old men were drawn to my younger, more 'perfect' body. I was one of the madam's prized possessions, and she wasn't about to let me go."

Closing her eyes, tears began streaming down her face. I pulled her into a hug and whispered, "I'm so sorry you went through all of this."

When her breathing evened out, she pulled back to wipe her tears. When she met my gaze again, she continued, "By the age of fifteen, I was no closer to the freedom I had been after than when I started. When I brought it up, she continuously put it off, making excuses as to why she couldn't grant it. For several years, I felt like there was no way out, and I contemplated killing myself. My mom was never aware of what the madam was asking me to do, but she didn't seem to care either. The only thing that mattered to her was the family she had found in the other workers in the brothel. But there was no room for me within that family.

"One day, I left for a contract Madam Tanith had placed on the northern lord of Maiviraea. Wandering through the woods, I found a large cave at the base of the Kolathus mountains. Curiosity got the best of me, and I entered it, finding the portal that led to these woods. I explored for a few days and got acclimated to the land. When I walked through the portal, it was autumn, and the trees had just started changing. It was mesmerizing compared to the way it happens in Caellaias. As much as I just wanted to rest and enjoy this new place I'd found, Madam Tanith would certainly be sending someone after me, so I went back to formulate a plan.

"When I returned to Caellaias, I finished my journey to the capital of northern Maiviraea, Rilias. While I wandered the capital searching for the lord, I stopped for food. There was a small tavern I went to every time I was in the capital called 'The Sollamthus Palace.' As I sat there waiting for my food, a woman approached me and asked if she could sit with me. I wasn't sure who she was, but I felt at ease the moment she sat down. Her floral scent told me she was a faerie. When I asked how I could help her, she smiled and said, 'You should be asking how *I* can help *you,* my dear.'

"When I asked who she was, she claimed she was a distant relative of the royal family but refused to tell me any more than that. After that, I tried to wave her off, thinking she wanted something from me in return, but then she told me she could help me escape, and my world stopped. I hadn't told her anything about my situation at that point, so I became defensive. After laughing, she explained that one of her powers was sensing distress, and if she touched me, she could see the cause. When she offered to help me again, I asked what she wanted, and she told me that freeing me was her repayment. I was confused, but I went along with it. I couldn't live the life I had anymore.

"Using her glamour magic and other resources, we found a deceased being, glamoured it to look like me, gave it my magical trail for a few weeks, and covered mine for a few days so I could escape to the home I live in now. I've been in contact with a few people who've told me Madam Tanith believed the corpse was me and showed no remorse for the potential that she pushed me to commit suicide. My mom, on the other hand, supposedly still grieves for me. To my knowledge, no one has ever tried to come looking for me. Because of everything I went through at that brothel, I vowed that I would never force myself onto someone again," Maeyve finished in a whisper.

We sat in silence as I processed everything. After she had a moment to compose herself, I whispered, "Maeyve, I'm sorry. I have a question, though. The way you explained everything seems like it's been a long time. You don't look to be a day over your mid-20s. May I ask how old you are?"

Maeyve didn't look back at me when she answered, "I'm around seventy years old. When we reach the age of twenty, we don't really age much and can live for thousands of years."

"Wow. Do you ever wish you could go back but live a different life?"

Maeyve huffed and responded, "No, I really don't. I enjoyed the scenery of the areas I visited, but it was an awful place to be for me. Even if I went back, too many people could recognize me. I was never truly happy until I moved to these woods –"

"Wait," I interrupted. "How long have you been here in your home?"

She looked up at me. "I've been out here for about fifty years."

I felt tears begin to well up as I processed everything she had been through. Without thinking, I pulled her into a hug. I felt guilty for how I had treated her. After hearing her story, I started to feel like I could understand her more—understand how much my accusations had hurt her.

I reached up to caress Maeyve's cheek, urging her to look at me, and whispered, "I'm so sorry for how I treated you yesterday. I really should have taken the time to listen to you. I was just scared and needed to process everything. Thank you for sharing your story with me." After a few beats of silence, another question popped into my head. "I am curious about how you're able to survive out here. How do you get food, clothes, and toiletries?"

Maeyve smiled. "Well, I was connected with one other being from Caellaias, who's been hidden among humans for decades. He used to give me odd jobs and, in exchange, provided me with food and necessities. If I didn't need anything, I would request money in exchange for my services. Unfortunately, he left the area recently to protect his growing family."

# Chapter Twenty-Seven

## Anevae

We ate dinner that night in silence after she finished her story. I stole glances between bites, but after a while, I couldn't take the silence anymore. I placed my hand on hers, hoping that it would be comforting if she felt the buzz between us.

When she looked at me quizzically, I said, "I just want to make sure you're okay."

She gave me a sad smile. "I'm fine. As much as I hate talking about my past, you needed to know."

Lowering my eyes, I pushed the remaining food around in my bowl. "Can I ask you something?"

"Anything, Anevae," she replied.

After taking a deep breath, I looked at her and asked, "What is it like for you when you seduce someone else?"

Stuttering, she answered, "Uh, well, umm. It's been a long time since I've done it. When I used it all those years ago, it felt like a burning sensation throughout my whole body, but not one that would hurt you, more like one that would warm you just to the edge of pain. It's similar to standing a little too close to a fire. It's arousing for the succubus, too, but I got used to fighting off that feeling after many years."

I chewed my lip before blurting, "Will you use it on me? So I can know what it's like?"

Maeyve sighed and removed her hand from mine. "Are you sure you want to do that? When it happens, I can't control your reaction. Hell, I might not even be able to control my own since it's been so long. I don't want to have sex with you just because you want to see what my abilities can do."

Placing my fork down, I stood from my chair and slowly walked around the island to where she sat. Looking her dead in the eyes, I whispered, "I wouldn't have asked if I weren't sure." Caressing her cheek, I planted a soft kiss on her lips. When I tried to pull back, she slid her arms around my waist and pulled me closer to deepen the kiss. Wedging myself between her legs, I wrapped my arms around her neck and tangled my fingers in her silky hair. After a few moments, she pulled back. Still keeping me close, she frowned.

"I hate using this ability. I haven't used it since I left Maiviraea. Even using my calming ability the other day on you was experimental and felt strange. I've had no reason to use any of my abilities in a very long time," she whispered as she looked into my eyes.

"You don't have to show me, but I want to know everything about you. You wouldn't be forcing yourself onto me; I'm asking for this. You can think of it as an... experiment. But you don't have to do it if you're uncomfortable," I reassured her.

She gave me a small smile that didn't reach her eyes and nodded. "Alright. I can show you, but be warned that things may move quickly when we do this."

I took a deep breath and slid my arms from around her neck to back up. She released me and placed her hands in her lap. Closing her eyes, she took a deep breath of her own.

When she opened her eyes, they were fixed directly onto mine. Her irises were the brightest orange I had ever seen, similar to that of an early morning sunrise. An intense pulsing began in my center, and a fierce heat spread throughout my body. I let out a small gasp and quickly closed the gap between us. Our lips collided, and an intense fire erupted throughout my body, causing me to moan against her mouth. A kiss wasn't enough to satiate the desire coursing through me.

The next thing I knew, I was in her arms with my legs wrapped around her waist. She moved faster than I'd ever seen someone move as she sprinted up the stairs and threw me down on my bed, the breath knocked out of me by the force.

She stood back and took a few steps away from the bed. Through gritted teeth, she said, "If you want to stop, you need to say so now. You need to know that I will not be gentle if we continue. This is your only warning, and I need you to answer quickly because I cannot hold myself back for long."

Unable to speak, I nodded furiously. Her last bit of restraint snapped as she reached for my pants and aggressively pulled them off. Then, she ripped off my panties and skimmed her hand up my thigh, straight to my soaking wet center. She wasn't gentle, and she gave no warning before she thrust two fingers deep into me, eliciting a scream from deep within my chest as I gripped the comforter tightly. She pumped her fingers in and out vigorously, and my back arched off the bed. She seemed to be able to find all the right spots to drive me wild. As she continued, she bit the inside of my thigh multiple times before her mouth descended onto my clit, and I screamed even louder. I reached down, grabbing a fist full of her hair as her free hand snaked under my leg to grip my hip tightly. Her nails dug into my flesh, breaking the skin. The pain mixed with pleasure had me tumbling over the edge into the most intense climax I'd ever experienced.

Maeyve continued pumping her fingers in and out of me until my shaking stopped. Once I released her hair, she lifted her eyes to meet mine. They were still a vibrant orange, which I was beginning to think was her tell that she was aroused. She had barely removed her fingers from my still pulsing core when I lunged toward her and began undressing her. With all of her clothes off, I hungrily kissed her, turning her so her back was to the bed, and shoved her down.

"You're not the only one who can be rough. I have a few ideas. Stay here," I ordered as I removed my shirt.

Retreating to my walk-in closet, I found the small box I sought and carried it back to the bedroom. Maeyve sat up, curious about what I was doing. When I opened it, the color of her eyes intensified. Inside were the sex toys I'd accumulated over the years. Shuffling through it, I found the two things I was looking for: a pair of thick leather handcuffs and a vibrating wand.

Taking the cuffs, I reached for Maeyve's hands, securing them tightly. When they were secured, I pushed her back on the bed and positioned her hands above her head. "You move those hands, and I will leave you on this bed, begging for me to fuck you as I tie your legs to the frame so you can't move an inch. Do you understand?" Standing over her, I gave her a sly grin, and she shivered in response. Swiping her tongue out over her lips, she nodded. "Good girl."

As I skimmed my hands down her body, my mouth followed, planting a trail of kisses toward her center. When I reached her bikini line, I skipped over it and went down to her knee, where I started the trail upward and spread her legs slowly. Reaching the middle of her thigh, I bit it hard. Maeyve let out a loud gasp and arched her back. Switching over to the other side, I did the same thing. As I approached her center, she began breathing heavier with each inch I gained.

Reaching the apex of her thighs, I thrust three fingers deep inside her and slowly moved them in and out as she screamed my name. With my free hand, I reached for the vibrating wand and turned it on. With a feather-light touch, I dragged the wand down her neck to her chest and around each nipple, then I moved to her leg. As I trailed from her knee to her bikini area, her moans intensified. Once I reached the top of her thigh, I adjusted the hand that was pumping in and out so I could press the tip of the wand to her clit. She screamed as soon as the wand made contact. Smirking, I moved my fingers inside her faster, rubbing that spot deep inside that drove her crazy. Her back arched higher and higher as her screams progressively got louder. Her body vibrated with pleasure as she came crashing over the edge, repeatedly screaming my name.

I continued until her shaking ceased. Turning off the wand, I threw it to the other side of the bed, pulled my fingers from inside of her, and licked them clean. Then, I climbed on top of her, straddling her. Like the good girl she was, her hands were still above her head.

Leaning down, I whispered in her ear, "You taste so good I could eat your pussy for an eternity and never get tired of it." Sitting up, I reached for the cuffs on her hands and murmured, "You listened like such a good girl. Are you pleased with your prize?"

When her hands were free, she sat up and wrapped her arms around my midsection, kissing me softly before answering, "That was amazing. I've never used one of those things, but I loved it."

Looking over, she opened the box of sex toys that was still on the bed. I blushed and reached to close it, but she stopped me.

"There's no need to be embarrassed. I'm just curious. These things are new to me. We didn't have any of these back in Maiviraea, and I haven't been with anyone since I was in the brothel."

"Wait. Did you just say I'm the first person you've had sex with in at least fifty years?" When she nodded, I shook my head in disbelief. "There's absolutely no way."

Maeyve giggled and glanced back at me. "Just because it's been that long doesn't mean I don't know how to use my abilities to make you feel good. Pleasure is ingrained into a succubus. Most succubi use the pleasure all for themselves, but some of us are more selfless than that and will use our intuition or even our abilities to please others."

"This is why I want to get to know you better. And I mean all of you," I said.

After kissing Maeyve quickly, I got off her lap and walked toward the bathroom. Turning back to where she sat, I motioned for her to follow me. I started a bath for us, and we continued exploring each other's bodies before finally washing up.

When we were done, I did my nightly routine and joined Maeyve in my bed. Cuddling up to her, I quickly fell asleep.

# Chapter Twenty-Eight

## Maeyve

After breakfast the next morning, I headed to my cabin for the rest of my clothes. I wasn't lying when I said I couldn't bear the thought of leaving Anevae's side. Being with her made me feel more comfortable since the ward around her home was down.

As soon as I walked out the door to leave, I felt eyes on me. Inhaling deeply, I caught the scent of leather and tarragon. Damn, vampire. I needed to come up with a way to get rid of him. He was a nuisance, and he frightened Anevae. He was the reason she would no longer step foot outside.

Anger pumped through my veins as I crept down the stairs, looking around for any hint of him. I'd have gladly killed him if given the chance. Unfortunately, a vampire could only be killed by decapitation or a wooden stake to the heart; catching a vampire off guard and decapitating them was difficult as they were always on edge and vigilant of their surroundings. Vampires were well aware of their weaknesses and only became vulnerable when they were starved. As they grow hungrier, they become weaker and slower. Seeing a starved vampire was like seeing a rabid animal; they bit everything and anyone in sight, just trying to get some blood.

A glimpse of movement to my right caught my attention, darting into the forest. Bounding down the stairs, I threw off piece after piece of clothing before shifting and sprinting toward the movement. As soon as I reached the tree line, I inspected the ground where I found footprints. The vampire's scent was strong there.

Irritation flowed through me as I followed the scent deeper into the forest, keeping my other senses on high alert and using an abundance of caution. A couple of twigs broke ahead. Then I spotted him. He stood about twenty feet away, waiting for me to approach him.

Snarling, I bared my teeth at the vampire. A smile spread across his face, and he chuckled deeply. "The king is getting very impatient. If she doesn't come to Caellaias within the next week, I'll have to take more drastic measures to get her out. Hmmm, that sounds tempting, actually. She can't stay in that house forever. The clock is ticking, foxy!"

A growl rumbled in my chest as I snapped out at him. We didn't know what the king wanted with Anevae besides the fact that she was his granddaughter, but the vampire would take her over my dead body. She wasn't his, nor was she the king's property. She barely knew anything about the kingdom of Caellaias.

His bright red eyes locked onto mine. "You're so fucking annoying. I wish I could just fucking kill you already. You're disgusting, and you don't deserve her."

Baring my teeth at him again, I barked and snarled as I prowled closer.

Rolling his eyes, he let out a sigh. "Would you just fuck off? I'm going, alright? Stupid bitch." Then, he ran off in the direction of the portal.

When he was out of sight, I scurried home to get dressed again and gather my remaining clothes. Eventually, I'd have to buy more, especially if I kept ruining the ones I had.

After stuffing everything into one of my few duffel bags, I rushed out the door to get back to Anevae. I was sure she was getting worried as I'd been gone for a bit. When I walked out the door, I looked for any signs of the vampire in case he had followed me home. No scents or sounds caught my attention, so I continued to Anevae's cabin.

Her face was plastered to the window, searching for me. I smiled as I approached, and a look of relief washed over her face when her eyes landed on me. The curtain fell closed, and she jerked the door open, ushering me inside.

Once we were safely inside, I pulled her into a tight embrace. Even though I knew she wouldn't leave the house, I was glad to see her waiting for me. Resting her head on my shoulder, she kissed my neck softly.

"I was worried about you," she whispered against my skin. After a few more moments, she released me and took a step back. "Is everything okay?" She asked as if she didn't want to know the answer.

Smiling back at her, I lightly kissed her temple. "You don't need to worry about me, but I appreciate that you do. Everything is alright now."

"Now? It wasn't before? Was the vampire out there?" Anevae asked, concern lacing her voice as her pupils dilated and her breathing picked up.

I sighed and met her gaze. "He was out there, but he's gone. Just breathe. I won't let anything happen to you; I promise. What are our plans for the day?"

Anevae scoffed as she looked away from me. "We have a lot we can do around here, especially since you've never seen most of the movies I own. I need to check in with my sister at some point, though. She didn't call me last night like she promised. I need to update her on everything that happened yesterday. I think she's skeptical about everything that's going on. We discussed involving our parents, but I'm really irritated with them right now. How do I know they won't try to take over and move me away from here? Or hide me away again? I'm no longer a child."

"You will always be their child, and they will always want to protect you, but I understand your frustration. They should have told you and prepared you for being on your own; they can't treat you like a child because you aren't. You're an adult whether they like it or not. They need to treat you as such."

When she turned back to me, the sadness was evident on her face. I could understand the feeling of disappointment and betrayal as I'd felt it from my mother many years before, back when she chose the family she found in the brothel over her own daughter. Your parents are supposed to protect you from danger and prepare you to take care of yourself; our parents had let us down, each in different ways. While my mother abandoned me and I'd never known my father, her parents neglected to prepare her for the world they ran from. They had to have known they couldn't keep her from it forever.

"I'm sorry this is happening to you, and you feel like you can't turn to your parents for help when you need them," I whispered. "Why don't you pick a movie that will cheer us up? I'll grab us some drinks and maybe make some popcorn if there's any left."

She smiled and nodded, then began searching for a movie as I headed to the kitchen. I found the last bag of popcorn, popping it into the microwave before getting us some drinks. We would watch this movie, and then we'd have to work on a plan. We needed to figure out what the king wanted with her, but I wasn't sure how we'd manage it. My eyes began to burn as tears welled to the surface. My heart ached for Anevae and the betrayal she was feeling. And for the first time in a long time, I allowed myself to feel sorry for the younger version of myself who just wanted her family to love her.

# Chapter Twenty-Nine

## *Anevae*

Maeyve and I spent the next week inside, talking, watching movies, and enjoying each other's company. I still refused to go outside, fearful the vampire would show up and attempt to take me again. Every day, I questioned why my dad wanted to keep Eiri and me from knowing about our heritage—*their* heritage. The only thing besides Maeyve that made this process any easier was the stories my mom told my sister and me as children.

Eiri checked in with me every morning, but I got concerned when I didn't hear from her on the morning of the seventh day. When Maeyve and I sat down for lunch, I messaged Eiri. When she didn't answer by that evening, I tried to call her, but it went straight to voicemail.

When I expressed my concern to Maeyve, she reminded me that my sister and I would go days without speaking to each other. While I knew she was right, I had a feeling in my gut that something wasn't right. What if the vampire had gotten her?

Maeyve explained that vampires didn't like this realm and would likely stay away from the city, so my sister was safer there. When I relented, she assured me we would check on Eiri the next day if we couldn't get ahold of her. Then, we headed for bed.

As soon as I woke up the next morning, I tried to call Eiri. It went straight to voicemail again. Anxious about Eiri's silence, I texted my mom to see if she'd heard from her before I freaked out completely.

> *Good morning! Have you heard from Eiri?*

> Good morning. I haven't. Is everything okay?

> I haven't heard from her in a couple of days now, so I just thought I'd see if you had. I wasn't sure what she had planned for the last few days.

> Maybe you can check on her? She was supposed to have an interview yesterday, but that's all I know about.

> Strange. She would have told me how the interview went.

As I sent the message, my heart sunk deep in my chest. Eiri wouldn't have missed one of her interviews unless something had happened, and if something had happened, she would have told me about it. *I should have listened to my gut. Something is absolutely wrong.*

As I set my phone down, my heart began to race, and my thoughts spiraled. If the vampire got her, I'd never forgive myself. I couldn't stay in this cabin if that were the case, but the idea of going outside had my anxiety heightened again.

Maeyve must have sensed my panic as she darted out of the bathroom, wrapped in a towel and still soaking wet. She kneeled next to the bed and asked, "What's wrong? Did your sister answer you?"

A lump was stuck in my throat, but I managed to answer her, "I texted my mom to see if she had heard from Eiri, and she hadn't heard from her either. I'm really concerned, but I still don't think I can bring myself to leave the house right now." Meeting her gaze, I continued, "I'm sorry to ask, but can you help me check on her?"

Still holding her towel with one hand, she reached up with the other and caressed my cheek. "I will always be here to help if you need it, and you never need to feel bad about asking for my help. Let me get dressed, and I'll head out to check on your sister. I know how much she means to you and how devastated you'd be if something happened to her."

After kissing my forehead, she lifted my eyes to meet hers and gave me a soft smile before retrieving clothes from the closet. She'd hung the few outfits she brought from her home there. As I'd guessed, her wardrobe consisted mainly of black with occasional specks of color.

Hurrying back to where I sat, she pulled me in for a tight embrace. I wrapped my arms around her neck and squeezed, nuzzling my face into her neck.

"I'll be back as soon as possible. Everything will be okay," she murmured before kissing my neck. After a few moments, she drew back. "Don't worry about me. No matter what, I'll always return to you."

Offering her a half smile, I nodded and closed my eyes. "Okay. Please be careful. I wouldn't forgive myself if something happened to you. I promise I'm working on making myself go outside." Squeezing my eyes tightly, a tear streamed down my cheek. But, before I could reach up and clear it, Maeyve was wiping it away with a quick flick of her thumb.

I felt her warm breath as she brought her forehead to mine. "Everything will be okay, I promise. I'll be quicker than you know, okay?"

I grabbed one of her wrists, pulled her palm to my lips, and kissed it gently. "Thank you."

She kissed my forehead again and brushed her thumb over my cheek before retreating downstairs. Shortly after, I heard the door shut. Feeling frustrated, I rubbed my eyes and took a deep breath. I needed to go downstairs and lock the door. It wasn't like the vampire could get in, but who knew what else was out there and the rules they followed? I scoffed at the thought before stomping down the stairs.

After I locked the door, I forced myself to watch Forensic Files, one of my comfort shows. A knock at the front door startled me. *Did Maeyve forget something?* I crept toward the door, trying not to make any sound.

A window at the front of the house gave me a full view of the porch. With trembling hands, I reached toward the curtain and pulled it back only as far as I needed to see who was there. To my surprise, there was no one. My SUV was the only vehicle in the driveway. *Am I being paranoid? Was there actually a knock?*

As I returned to my TV show, I came up with explanations for the sound. Maybe a bird flew into the window, or a nut fell onto my car. That had to be it. I simply misheard. Any explanations I had talked myself into were shattered when another knock sounded at the door.

Brows furrowed, I stomped to the window again and peered out. Again, no one stood on the porch; my vehicle was the only one in the drive. There was no way I was imagining the knock. Just as I was about to sit back down, I saw something fluttering on the door. *What the hell?*

Turning around, I tried to find something to arm myself with. If there were someone, or something, waiting for me on the other side just out of view, I wouldn't be caught completely off guard again. I hurried into the kitchen and found the biggest knife possible. *Would this even hurt a vampire if I stabbed them? For fuck's sake, what is wrong with me?*

Stomping to the door, I cracked it open and saw a piece of paper taped to it. Reaching out, I ripped it off and slammed the door shut.

Leaning my back against the door, I read the letter. On the thick cream-colored parchment, in scrawling black letters, it read:

> If you ever want to see your sister again, come to Castle Rilvara. Your pet can bring you here but do not involve your parents. If you do, the consequences will be dire. Your grandfather, King Casimir, is looking forward to your arrival, and I've been dying to get my hands on you again. We will be waiting, albeit impatiently, but we look forward to you joining us.
>
> You have three days, Princess.
>
> -Emrhys

I was too late. He took her. Dropping to the floor, I went into a full-blown panic attack. I couldn't focus, and I could hear my heart beating in my ears. My breathing grew ragged, and I began to feel dizzy. I had to find a way to get myself out of this house and to my sister.

Trying to calm down, I skimmed the note again. *Emrhys—so that was the name of the vampire actively trying to ruin my life.* He was right; Maeyve *could* help me get to Caellaias and save Eiri. But how could I possibly ask that of her after everything she had told me? There had to be another way.

As my breathing returned to normal, rapid footsteps ascended the porch steps. I scrambled to my feet and rushed to the window to see who it was. Maeyve was already at the door, pounding on it and looking frantic.

Clenching the note, I hurried to open the door for her. Relief washed over Maeyve's face when she saw me, but I started crying again as soon as my gaze met hers. She hurried in, slammed the door shut, and pulled me into her arms. She carried me over to the couch, sat, and held me tight.

"What happened?" she whispered.

Pulling back, I handed her the note that was now crumpled and damp from my clammy hands. "He took her. She's in Caellaias! I have to get her back, but I don't know how to get there, and you're the only person who can help me. How could I ever ask you to return to that terrible place?"

"Take some deep breaths. We'll find a way to bring her back, even if that means we have to go to Caellais and get her. I will do anything to bring her back to you, even if it means going back there," Maeyve whispered into my hair as she rocked me.

Taking deep breaths, as she suggested, I sat up and looked at Maeyve, who was waiting patiently. As she looked over my face, she had a deep sadness in her eyes.

"You weren't gone very long. What happened?" I asked, not sure I wanted to know the answer.

She hesitated for a moment before answering. "I found your sister's car, abandoned, down by my house and immediately knew something was wrong, so I came right back."

Tears welled in my eyes again. *Eiri's car was abandoned. By Maeyve's house. Was she coming to check on me when she encountered the vampire?*

None of that really mattered. He had taken her, and I needed to bring her back home.

"We will get her back. Can I see the note?"

When I handed her the note, I climbed out of her lap. I paced in front of her while she studied it. As she finished reading, she growled and threw the note on the couch beside her.

She stood, walked over to me, and pulled me into her arms. "This vampire—Emrhys—seems like a fucking asshole. I will do everything in my power to make sure he never touches you again. Never. Again." Huffing out a breath, she nuzzled into my hair and took a deep breath.

"You said there's a portal in these woods?" I asked.

Maeyve stepped back and gave me a sad look. "Yes. There is."

"Can we go into Maiviraea and make our way to the castle from there?" I asked, hopeful for the first time since I found the note.

"I think that's the only way we'll get to Eirvanna without traveling elsewhere. Caellaias has many outlets in the Earth realm, but they are spread far and wide. We would risk time going elsewhere. My biggest concern is that Emrhys is likely using that route to get to Eirvanna. He could try to intercept us on our way to the castle."

"I don't want you to go to Caellaias just because you want to protect me. I can try –"

Maeyve leaned in close, making sure I met her gaze. With furrowed brows, she spoke, "All you have to do is say the word, and I'm right there. I don't care what I went through in Caellaias. If you need me, I'll always be there. We've only known each other for a short time, but being with you brings so much happiness into my life; I cannot imagine a life without you anymore."

Tears welled in my eyes as I whispered, "You bring about feelings in me that I've never experienced before. I've never been this connected to someone. I get this sense of peace and unending happiness when I'm around you; you calm every storm that has been wreaking havoc in my mind for so many years. I don't ever want you to leave because I'm afraid of how I'll feel if you do. But I don't want you to feel obligated to go to Caellaias with me and regret it."

She tilted my chin up lightly and softly kissed my lips. Then, she placed her forehead against mine and murmured, "I will never leave your side unless I am forced to or you tell me to. I will never regret anything I do as long as you're by my side."

Smiling, I pulled back from her hold. A tear rolled down her cheek, and I wiped it away. "I think I'm beginning to fall in love with you," I admitted softly.

# Chapter Thirty

# *Anevae*

The next day went by in a blur as we devised a plan to rescue my sister and packed for our journey to Caellaias. I was nervous about leaving but knew I had to find Eiri. Momma's stories of my grandfather made him sound cruel, and Maeyve's impressions of him weren't much different. I couldn't wrap my head around what he wanted with us—especially since we were half-breeds. Of course, I also had to create a diversion for my parents so they didn't rush to the area and not find us, so I texted my mom.

*Hey Momma. I went to check on Eiri, and everything was fine.*

After receiving her message, I scheduled several texts to her in case we weren't back in time. They detailed what had happened since I moved in, minus the details of my relationship with Maeyve, where we were, and how we'd gotten there.

When that was done, Maeyve and I sat down to work on our plan. She grabbed a piece of paper and a pen so she could draw a map and explain in more detail how we'd get to the castle. As she drew each portion, I remembered where each territory was and the beings that inhabited it. In the center was Eirvanna, home of the fae; to the north was Maiviraea, home of the shifters; to the east was Baeruil, home of the angels; to the south was Lamatorre, home of the vampires; to the west was Kaeuil, home of the demons.

After the territories were laid out, she went into more detail, drawing the forest and the Kolathus mountains. To signify the location of the portal, she circled an area where the trees meet the mountains. As she did this, she warned me that shifters guard the portal, but since we were both beings from Caellaias, they wouldn't pay too much attention to us.

Then, she drew the castle, and my heart sank. "Please tell me we won't have to walk the entire way." Knowing that a map could drastically differ from the actual distance, I was hoping she was misjudging the distance.

"Well, I don't think we have much choice. I don't have the money or resources to commission a carriage ride. I also need to stay as hidden as possible in Maiviraea; the last thing we need is for someone to recognize me and report my return to Madam Tanith."

"Okay. That makes sense. But how long will it take us to walk to the castle from the portal?" I asked hesitantly.

Maeyve bit her lip before responding, "A couple of days at least."

"There's gotta be another way!"

"I don't think there is, Anevae."

"Fuck it. You know what? Whatever. I just want to bring my sister home, where she belongs."

"We will."

"Is there anything else that will complicate the journey?"

"There shouldn't be. It should be pretty straightforward once we reach Eirvanna."

"Okay, well, let's round everything up and get out of here," I said, determined to get everything going as quickly as possible; the sooner we got there, the better.

About half an hour later, I stood staring at the door with everything ready to go. I was determined to save my sister, but the fear I'd developed of being outside crept up the moment I thought about opening the door.

"It's okay, Anevae. You can do this," Maeyve said in an encouraging voice.

Taking a step forward, I gripped the doorknob, and my heart felt like it was beating out of my chest. *It'll be okay. We have to get Eiri.* Then, I took a deep breath and slowly pulled the door open. As soon as I felt the breeze from outside, I got dizzy and slammed the door shut. I began shaking uncontrollably, and Maeyve came up behind me, wrapping her arms around my waist.

"It'll be okay. I know you're scared. Take a few more deep breaths, clear your mind, and try again," she whispered in my ear.

Doing as she said, I placed my hand over hers and squeezed when I was ready to try again. This time, I got as far as stepping one foot outside, but then I saw movement in the woods and scrambled back inside.

Maeyve approached me again and wrapped me in a tight embrace. "Don't push yourself too hard. This is a real fear that you're working so hard to conquer."

A tear slid down my cheek more out of frustration than fear. "I feel like every time I come rushing back through that door, I'm failing my sister."

"You're not though. You're working through your fears to get to your sister. Give yourself some credit for that."

With a sigh, I looked into her eyes. "You're right. Thank you for your patience with me. I truly appreciate it."

Maeyve did a quick sweep of the perimeter, checking for the vampire or other beings. I was grateful to hear her say she hadn't found any. *It's now or never. Get your ass out there and get to Eiri.*

As I approached the door, anxiety built again. Taking one last deep breath, I ripped open the door and rushed out onto the porch, but I didn't stop there; I ran into the grass and all the way to the tree line before I stopped. Maeyve was with me within seconds.

"Wait! Did you –" I began to ask frantically.

Standing before me, she held my shoulders. "I closed the door behind me and locked it on the way out. The house will be safe." Then, she smiled softly and said, "You're doing great. I'm proud of you. Let's go."

I squeezed Maeyve's hand and leaned in for a quick kiss. "Thank you. You've been so amazing and helpful throughout this entire process. I don't know how I could ever repay you for everything you've done for me."

"You don't need to thank me. I know I keep saying it, but I would do anything for you. I felt a connection the first time I saw you, but I didn't want to push it. I'm thankful every day that you came to my cabin to introduce yourself to me because if the roles were reversed, I wouldn't have taken that first step. If I'm honest, I think I fell in love with you the moment I first met you. I know I've lived much longer than you, but I've never experienced love–not even from my mother. You're a strong, beautiful, amazing woman who deserves the world. I don't deserve you, but I want to be selfish and keep you anyway. I've never felt this way with anyone else, and I don't think I ever will again."

A tear rolled down my cheek as I listened to Maeyve. I could feel how much she meant every word. When she was done, I wiped my tears and pulled her in for a deep kiss. As we separated, I glanced back at my cabin. I was determined to bring my sister home.

Maeyve stared at me with a question in her eyes, and I nodded. I was ready. She laced our fingers and led the way deeper into the woods.

A few miles into the trek, we came across a steep incline. Instead of going up the slope, we went around it. Several hundred feet ahead was the opening to a cave.

Closing her eyes and taking a deep breath, she squeezed my hand. We were nervous to go into this place for two completely different reasons, but we had each other, which helped calm my nerves.

As I looked into the cave, Maeyve stepped in front of me. "Things in Caellaias are very different from here. Some things are similar, but the protectors of the realm do what they can to avoid contamination between worlds."

I nodded, and we moved into the cave. When everything went black, I blinked rapidly, and my stomach roiled. The sensation made me pause, but Maeyve squeezed my hand and ran her thumb over mine.

"I've got you," she whispered, and that was all the encouragement I needed to keep going.

# Chapter Thirty-One

# Anevae

Just as quickly as the light in the cave vanished, a faint light appeared ahead. The closer we got to the end of the tunnel, the more of the landscape ahead came into focus. At first, all I could see was a sea of different shades of red. I blinked, my eyes adjusting to the light, and my jaw dropped. Everything was so vibrant. Letting go of Maeyve's hand, I rushed forward toward the mouth of the cave.

More and more details came into focus; there were a multitude of colors. They were mesmerizing. As Momma described when we were young, the leaves were a rich red, almost the color of ripe tomatoes. None of the leaves were the purple Momma had mentioned they would turn during the autumn-like season of Caellaias. The tree bark matched the color of the mahogany wood used to build my cabin, and the grass was the most luscious green I'd ever seen. Despite not having seen the kingdom for several decades, Momma's descriptions were so perfect it felt like I had been there before.

Maeyve came up beside me and intertwined our fingers once more. "I know this is all new and different for you, but please stay close to me and be careful. I don't think I would be able to live with myself if something happened to you. The animals in this area can be unpredictable, sometimes acting without thinking. When you're ready, we need to go this way," she said softly as she pointed toward the left.

A deep growling came from our right. Maeyve immediately shoved me behind her as she began to crouch and growl in return. My heart started pounding as I searched for the source of the sound. A large black and white fox stood on the other side of Mayeve, just a few yards beyond the mouth of the cave. Something about the animal felt familiar.

Maeyve straightened up and laughed. "No freaking way. Calliope! Is that you?" Maeyve asked as she began approaching the fox. "What the hell are you doing out here?"

The fox whimpered, and its ears flattened as it backed up. Maeyve stopped and got down on her knees. Lowering her head, I could hear her mumble, "I'm sorry, Calli."

The fox ran up, licked Maeyve's face, and darted further into the woods. Maeyve remained crouched on the ground, but the way her shoulders shook, I could tell she was crying. I walked up, knelt, and hugged her from behind to comfort her.

Rustling drew my attention to where the fox had disappeared. Instead of a fox, I found a woman staring at us. This was Calliope. She was tall and beautiful, resembling Maeyve in many ways. Her hair was the same mass of black curly waves, but hers had streaks of white instead of orange. Her honey-colored doe-eyes were similar to Maeyve's, and her lips were slightly thinner but still the perfect bow shape. Though they had a similar cute snubby-shaped nose, Calli's nostrils flared further out.

Slowly, Calli approached Maeyve and knelt beside her. I let go of Maeyve and sat back. They were familiar with each other, and I wanted to give them space. Calli reached out and placed her hand on

Maeyve's shoulder, but Maeyve quickly pulled her into a tight hug. Calli squeezed Maeyve back and nuzzled into the crook of her neck as she began to cry.

"I've missed you so much," Maeyve whispered.

"What are you doing here? Everyone thought you were dead. Where have you been?"

Maeyve let go of Calli to look her over. "Not much of our family cared what happened to me in that brothel, so they didn't need to know that I'm still alive. I'm glad to see you, though." Sniffling, she wiped her nose and looked around. "Are you on guard patrol?"

Calli nodded as she moved to stand. "Unfortunately, I am. Family duty, ya know?"

"Fuck family duty. You're barely of age! Why the hell would they place you on guard duty all the way out here? And alone at that!" Maeyve grumbled as she stood, turning to me. "Sorry, sweetheart; this is my cousin, Calliope. I'm sure you can see some similarities. The fox shifter genes are very prominent in our family."

Calli laughed. "I'm happy to see you haven't changed much since the last time I saw you, Maeyve." Gesturing over at me, she asked, "And who is this you have with you? She smells like a royal."

Sighing, Maeyve grabbed my hand and turned back to me, giving me a loving look. "It's a very long story, Calli. You cannot tell ANYONE, you hear me?" Maeyve glanced back at her cousin and gave her a severe stare. When Calli nodded, Maeyve continued, "Her name is Anevae. She's Princess Cordilaen's daughter."

Calli's eyes grew wide, and she stepped back a couple of paces but stopped. She cleared her throat, took a deep breath, and looked back at me. Giving me a small curtsy, she said, "I'm so sorry, Your Highness. I'm just shocked to hear that Princess Cordilaen had a daughter. She's been missing for a long time." Her face settled into a scowl. "Wait, who's your father? Is he a human?!"

Frustration bubbled deep in my gut. *What was with all the questions? What did it matter to her?*

Maeyve squeezed my hand, which helped ground me as she replied to her cousin's question, "Her father is Roarc, Lord Amaroc's second son who went missing around the same time as Princess Cordilaen."

Calli gasped, "Oh. King Casimir isn't going to like that. The royal family has always been purebred fae."

Irritation stirred again. "What the hell is so wrong with half-breeds?"

Calli glanced at her feet and mumbled, "I personally have nothing against half-breeds, but King Casimir is a firm believer in the idea that power comes from status; purebreds are considered the most powerful beings in his eyes. I don't completely agree with that idea, but King Casimir ostracized his eldest daughter because she fell in love with a being that was not another purebred fae. When she left, he had high hopes for your mother. After your mother disappeared, he was devastated.

"King Casimir is not of direct royal descent as he married into the family. His father was a High Lord. He is, of course, a purebred fae, but he does not possess the abilities the royals do. When Queen Ahmeira passed away, she took the possibility of there being any more royal children."

"So my mom and aunt are the only direct descendants of the queen that can pass down the royal abilities? Could that be why the king wants me? Is that why he took Eiri, too? Even with us being half-breeds, we can still pass down whatever special powers the royals do, right?" I asked, looking at Maeyve.

"Yes, your mom and aunt were the last ones known to possess the royal abilities. If you have these abilities, it is possible for you to give them to your children. But that would depend greatly on who you had children with and what their bloodline was like."

My concern about meeting my grandfather intensified. Everything was starting to make sense. When he couldn't get to my mom, he turned to the next best thing: my sister and I. He would never give up in his pursuit of finding his family, especially his daughter. Having

Eiri and me made that easier. He could lure my mom to him with her daughters in his possession.

I stood there, stuck in my thoughts, when Calli said, "Maeyve, you need to get out of here before anyone else sees you. My parents are out here patrolling, too. I can arrange for a carriage to take you both to the castle so you can get there quicker and avoid prying eyes, but be careful when you get there. I've heard that King Casimir has been quite brutal as of late. He may not take kindly to you accompanying his granddaughter as you, yourself, are a half-breed."

Just then, I had an idea. "If we don't have to go to the castle on foot, it won't take us as long to get there, right?" Maeyve nodded, and I continued, "Can we stop to see my other grandfather? Maybe he can help us get my sister back."

Calli burst out laughing as I finished. Confused, I glared at her. She cleared her throat when she caught me glaring and explained, "No offense, but you don't know Lord Amaroc. He's a traditional wolf shifter and has quite a temper. My guess is that your father ran away for a multitude of reasons. Sure, King Casimir was angry at Cordilaen, but Roarc was also arranged to be married. Your father is as good as dead to Lord Amaroc, which means he may not take kindly to you either."

My heart sank. I'd grown up thinking I had no grandparents, only to find out that both of my grandfathers seemed to be pompous asses who may not accept me, and at least one of my grandmothers was dead. There really was so much I had to learn about my life that my parents had kept from me.

With everything running through my mind, I didn't notice Maeyve was talking to me again until she caressed my cheek, pulling me from my spiraling thoughts.

She gave me a small smile and asked again, "Are you okay? I know this is a lot for you to deal with."

Tears welled in my eyes as I whispered, "No. I'm trying to process everything I've learned and understand more about my family that's been hidden from me. I'm in a strange place going to meet my grandfather—whom I didn't know existed until a few days ago—because he had my sister abducted."

"I understand. Everything will be okay." She gave me a light, swift kiss and grasped my hand again to lead me to where Calli had wandered.

Before we left the forest, Calli stopped to let another of the protectors know she'd be headed to Ceraias for the night and would see them later.

Calli said as we began our trek, "This trip is normally a lot faster in my fox form, but... Can you shift, Anevae?"

"I'm not sure yet. I've never tried," I said.

"I'm almost certain her mother was giving her suppressants. She doesn't even have access to her fae magic yet," Maeyve added.

"Hmm. Interesting. I'm sure you'll be able to. But I apologize in advance; this is going to be a long walk," Calli said.

Shrugging, I said, "I came into Caellaias expecting to have to walk to Castle Rilvara. You're already saving me from walking all the way there."

"Okay. We also likely won't reach my home until nightfall, so make sure to stay close to us. The fact that I could smell your royalty means many others will as we go through the cities. The royal family hasn't made an appearance outside of Eirvanna in centuries," Calli said.

"Why?" I asked, genuinely curious.

Calli looked at Maeyve before explaining, "Your grandfather wasn't the first one to think poorly of half-breeds. Many of the prior kings and queens believed that the fae were the superior race –"

"That doesn't make sense, though. Why would the king employ shifters and vampires to be guards of the castle? Wouldn't he want all of his guards to be fae?" I asked, confused.

A smirk appeared on Calli's face as she looked over at me. "I think I'll rather like you."

From there, we walked in silence. Once we left the woods, Calli took us through a few small towns. The little homes throughout them were simple and battered. But when we arrived in Ceraias, the homes were drastically different.

Even in the lamplight around the city, I could see that Calli's home was a small two-story house with a beautiful structure made of black bricks. The matching black roof was slanted, similar to the ones in the Earth realm. It was immaculate.

Calli ushered us in and showed us a room we could use for the night. After putting our things down, Calli found us something to eat, then went to find a map to Castle Rilvara. As we ate, Calli and Maeyve spoke about our trip to the castle while I sat quietly, still processing everything. When I was done, I excused myself and got ready for bed; it'd been a long day, and the next day wouldn't be much better.

# Chapter Thirty-Two

## *Anevae*

When the carriage arrived the next morning, Maeyve climbed in first with our belongings and helped me up. As I settled into my seat, I couldn't help but wonder aloud, "Maeyve, what if my grandfather doesn't accept me?"

Sitting across from me, she cupped my cheek and smiled softly. "We know he's not going to be pleased that you're a half-breed, but anyone would be crazy *NOT* to love and accept you, especially your grandfather. From everything I've heard, he adored your mom. I'm certain he'll adore you as well."

Returning the smile, I muttered, "Thank you. You're such an incredible woman. I've never met anyone like you, nor did I ever think I'd be treated like this in my life. Before you, I didn't think I deserved this kind of love; I thought I'd always be alone."

When the carriage began to move, Maeyve and I sat back in our respective seats, and I stared at her for a while. I didn't know what I'd done to deserve someone as amazing and perfect as her, but I never wanted to let her go. Then, I began to wonder what would happen to her when we got to the castle. She was a half-breed, and my grandfather wouldn't like that I was keeping one so close to me. She wasn't even part fae, either. It crossed my mind that he could dismiss her or force her out of the castle if he desired, but if he wanted me to stay for any length of time, he'd likely try to do everything he could to please me.

Maeyve dared a glance at me, and my gaze shifted to her plump, pink lips. Biting my lip piercing, I could only think about having those soft lips on mine. Just the thought of it had a pulse running through my center. Our eyes locked, and I couldn't handle it any longer. I crawled onto Maeyve's lap to straddle her. As our lips collided, an intense spark coursed throughout my entire body. I tangled my hands into her soft hair and pulled back, momentarily separating our lips.

Her beautiful orange eyes had darkened with desire. I needed her, and she needed me, too. Her hands fell to my hips and gripped tightly as she murmured my name. Smirking, I lowered my lips to her ear, trailing kisses down her neck. As I reached the crook, I licked my way back up. The soft moans coming from her lips caused the pulsing in my center to intensify tenfold.

Releasing her hair with one hand, I continued to kiss her neck, trailing my now free hand down her arm to her hip. Once I reached the hem of her shirt, I slid my fingers underneath it to her breast. As I lightly skimmed my fingertips over her now-hardened nipple, my deepest desires took over, and I bit down on her neck. This time, I wasn't soft about it. My canines pierced her skin, and her sweet blood coated my tongue, sending a comforting warmth through my body. She attempted to stifle a moan, and her grip tightened on my hips as she climaxed under me.

After a moment, I withdrew my teeth from her neck and sat back to meet her gaze. Licking my lips, I thought, *What did I just do?* She looked back up at me, breathing heavily as she slid her fingertips across my lower back. Her pupils had taken over her irises, and there was only a tiny slit of orange left.

Moments later, she had me on my back. Eyes wide, she reached up to her neck, where blood was still trickling from the wound my teeth left. Pulling her hand away, she saw the blood coating her fingers, and her mouth dropped open.

Still staring at her fingers, she mumbled, "We need to talk about this before this goes any further." Her voice was husky and full of lust. Licking her lips, she met my gaze again before continuing, "I know you didn't mean to, but you just initiated a mating bond with me. I've *never* heard of two women being mated. That's why I never stopped you from biting me; I didn't think this could happen. *Fuck.* I think we should stop. I wouldn't feel right completing the bond with you right now. You don't understand what that would mean," Maeyve said as she pulled away.

I instantly wrapped my arms around her neck to keep her close and smirked. "I may not understand it, but being mated to you doesn't sound so bad. I don't want us ever to be separated. Now, we can make sure that happens. What if this was always meant to happen?"

"Anevae, you don't understand. If we complete the bond, we will become physically and mentally unwell if we are separated for too long. There are too many unknowns going to the castle. Besides, your grandfather has enough power and resources that he could have our mate marks removed if he wanted to." She blinked back tears, and her voice cracked when she tried to start talking again, "I love you, and if this were under different circumstances, I may not be fighting it. I wonder if this means your magic is awakening. We need to discuss so many things before we go through with this."

Frowning, I considered her words before replying. "Maeyve, I love you. And I want you forever. My grandfather can have whatever opinion of our mating he wants, but I will fight for you until the end. He will not separate us; I'll make sure of it." I cupped her cheek. "I've already initiated the bond. Who knows what will happen if we don't finish what I started? Call me crazy, but I feel this was destined to happen."

Maeyve bit her lip, growled, and pushed herself out of my arms onto the seat opposite of me. She began running her fingers through her hair and bouncing her leg as she clenched her jaw, fighting with herself.

I clasped my hands together in my lap and dropped my gaze. I wasn't sure what to do or say. She just wanted to do what she thought was right. I appreciated her concern for me, but it was misplaced. The taste of her blood lingered in my mouth, and I touched my fingertips to my lips, replaying the way she came for me the instant it happened.

"Gods damn it, Anevae. You're not making this easy. I can smell your arousal from here. I want to be a good person right now, but I'm already hanging on by a thread. My body is begging me to complete the bond, but –"

"So do it," I purred, glancing back at her and biting my lip.

She sprung at me and straddled my lap. As she ground into me, she kissed my neck a couple of times before she bit me. A blazing fire spread through my body from where her teeth sunk into my skin. An orgasm hit me hard and fast as the fire wore off. I couldn't help but scream as waves of intense pleasure overcame me. Thankfully, the driver didn't seem to hear us or be affected by our sounds at least.

Maeyve retracted her teeth from my neck and hummed against my skin.

*Fuuuuck. Her blood tastes almost as good as her pussy.*

Her voice echoed in my mind, but her mouth wasn't moving. *What the fuck?* My eyes met hers as she sat up.

Giving me a sinister smile, I heard her voice in my head again. *Sweet Anevae, it's a perk of being mated. We can communicate telepathically, but sadly, we can't read each other's minds. This is going to be amazing. Imagine the pictures I can place into that mind of yours at the most inappropriate times.* A picture of me lying on my back, playing with my nipples while I had my head thrown back, was on full display for me.

"Maeyve!" I shrieked, and then I gasped. "Oh, my god. That's why my parents seem like they're having a full-blown conversation without saying a word!"

Maeyve giggled. Blood seeped from the wound on my neck and trailed toward the fabric of the seat. When I moved to sit up, she shoved me down and latched onto my neck again. She ran her tongue over the wound, then sat back up. I brushed my fingers over the wound, and my mouth popped open. The indents were still there, but the wounds had closed, and the bleeding had stopped. My gaze landed on Maeyve's neck. Hers had stopped bleeding on its own.

"Mates can heal each other's mating marks with their blood, but we shifters in the canine family also have saliva with healing properties," Maeyve said.

She rifled through our bags and retrieved a new shirt since hers was now soaked in blood. As she removed her shirt, my eyes roamed over her bare chest, which had a trail of blood from the mark to the swell of her breast. I stood and wrapped my arms around her waist before licking the blood trail clean, savoring the flavor of her.

"Your blood tastes as sweet as you smell, like vanilla and berries. What do I taste like?" I asked teasingly.

"You also taste sweet but floral, like chocolate and lilies almost, but your blood has an electric feeling to it," Maeyve claimed. "It could be from your magic or your lineage. Thank you for cleaning up the blood a little bit."

Kissing me lightly, she unraveled my arms from around her and finished cleaning her neck with her blood-stained shirt. When she finished, she put on her clean shirt and sat back down. I took the seat across from her again. She kissed my knuckles and then released my hand, relaxing against the seat to look out the carriage's window. Following suit, I stared out the window behind her as I thought about our mating and what that meant for us now.

We rode silently for a while, but when I least expected it, I heard Maeyve's voice in my head again. *What are you thinking?*

When she did that, I yelped and about jumped out of my skin. Quickly glancing back at her, I scowled. "I'm never going to get used to that."

Maeyve smiled and jested, "You will eventually, love. Especially if you're going to be stuck with me for the rest of our lives."

As I smiled, I thought of her lying on my island at home, completely naked. *Two can play that game, sweetheart.* I giggled.

"This is going to be way too much fun," Maeyve said, chuckling as she moved to sit beside me. Planting a quick kiss on my lips, she sighed. "I love you, Anevae. While I'm glad we're mated, I'm concerned about how your grandfather will react. Not only am I a half-breed, but I'm also another female."

Reaching up between us, I gripped her chin and gave her a small smile. "We will cross that bridge once we get there. Everything will be okay." Leaning in, I kissed her again, released her chin, and rested my forehead against hers. "I love you, too, Maeyve."

When we separated, I leaned my head on her shoulder and said, "Seeing as we'll be in this carriage for the rest of the day and night, why don't you tell me what you remember about Caellaias?"

Maeyve sighed but got comfortable and began telling me about her travels throughout Maiviraea. In between her stories, she asked me about my ventures through the human realm. We continued this cycle for hours.

Just as the sun began to set behind the mountains, she said, "It's getting late. You should try to get some sleep. I'm not tired quite yet."

She scooted over as far as she could and patted her lap. I laid down, hair splayed across it, and snuggled in.

While I lay there, I thought about my parents. If they were aware my sister and I were in Caellaias, they'd do whatever they could to get us home, but I didn't want to involve them unless I had to. I was still confused and hurt about why my dad would downplay Caellaias. Clearly, my mom wanted us to know about it. She likely knew they couldn't keep us from Caellaias forever, but my dad seemed to think he could protect us for the rest of our lives. I pondered whether that was the reason they got so upset when I said I'd be moving to the mountains. Did they know the portal was near my cabin? Was that how they escaped Caellaias?

Finally, my mind cleared enough that I fell into a deep, dreamless sleep, protected by my mate.

# Chapter Thirty-Three

## Maeyve

I absentmindedly stroked Anevae's hair as I stared out the carriage's window. After about twenty minutes, her breathing evened, and I knew she was asleep, comfortable, and safe in my lap. I let out a long sigh, leaned back, and closed my eyes.

There was so much going through my mind that I wasn't sure I'd be able to sleep. The biggest concern plaguing my mind was how the king would react to the news that I had mated his granddaughter. Would he be as stunned as I was that we were able to do so? Would he be disgusted by our union? Even if I weren't a half-breed, I couldn't provide Anevae with the heir he desperately desired. Same-sex relationships were common in Caellaias, but I'd never seen them publicly amongst the royal family.

It was within his power to separate us if he saw fit. I had heard rumors of magic users powerful enough to sever mate bonds, and I had no doubt that King Casimir would hire one if he were angry enough. Then, there was always the possibility that he would try to turn Anevae against me. I didn't think he would be successful. After all, Casimir had been so terrible to Cordilaen that she had fled the entire realm and lied to her children for decades.

King Casimir hadn't even bothered to try to talk to Anevae before he attempted to kidnap her. Sure, as king, he was used to getting his way, but a little diplomacy tends to go a long way. Did he just want to bring her to him so she wouldn't fight or question him? She likely wouldn't have understood what was going on and would have been scared out of her mind. Maybe he assumed that her parents had turned them against him, and this was the only way to get to her.

I wasn't even sure how he had found Anevae in the first place. She had barely been in her new home a week when Emrhys attempted to steal her away. He had to have some knowledge of the girls if he was able to locate her that quickly with the wards and Cordilaen's glamour magic.

Looking down, I admired the perfect woman lying in my lap. She looked so serene lying there, oblivious to what we could encounter when we entered the castle. She hadn't been exposed to this world like I had; she didn't understand how cruel some of these beings could be. During my time in Maiviraea, I'd heard how cruel her grandfather was from others, but had he changed since I'd been gone?

Tears welled in my eyes. For the first time in years, I was scared. I feared the happiness I found with Anevae would be ripped away from me, and I would feel the emptiness that plagued me when I fled from Caellaias all those years prior.

Continuing to stroke her hair with one hand, I moved the other to cup her rosy cheek. I would fight to keep her by my side at all costs. My life had started to turn around and mean something since she had entered it. My days no longer blurred together; every day was an adventure with her. I never, ever thought I'd find love after all the things I went through at the brothel.

One of my tears landed on her cheek, and I hurried to wipe it away. I didn't want to wake her. She needed the rest, and I didn't want her to worry about me; she had enough to worry about with her sister being taken.

Looking out the window again, I wiped the tears from my eyes. We were gaining distance from Ceraias, but the forest kept steady to the East. It extended into Eirvanna, stopping just outside the castle walls.

With Calli's estimations, we'd make it to Castle Rilvara by midday the following day. Running into her had been pure luck, but I was thankful for it nonetheless. I appreciated her help in arranging a carriage to get us to the castle. It kept us hidden from sight and sped up our travel significantly. Getting to Eiri quickly was critical. We both dreaded the long walk, but I knew she'd do whatever it took to get her sister home.

A few hours after the sun had set behind the horizon, I finally began feeling sleepy. Judging by the wide open fields ahead, we were nearing the border of Eirvanna, which meant we were about halfway to the castle. Anevae had barely stirred in my lap for the entirety of the ride; I was glad she was able to sleep so soundly.

My anxiety about entering the fae territory plagued me, preventing me from sleeping. I'd never been there and had very little interaction with the fae while in the brothel. One of the other women there was part fae, but she'd never lived in Eirvanna, and she had been abandoned as a child by her birth parents. Most clients who entered the brothel were shifters due to our location, but I'd heard the other women say the fae weren't often found outside Eirvanna. No one ever told me why, but I assumed it had to do with the status of the fae society.

When my heavy eyelids could no longer stay open, I rested my head against the side of the carriage. It was unlikely that we would encounter anyone this far from any of the cities, which was a comforting thought.

I slept lightly, awakening at every little sound, and when the sun began to rise, I was wide awake again.

# Chapter Thirty-Four

# *Anevae*

I woke up with my head in Maeyve's lap as she stroked my hair. Her eyes were fixated on something outside of the carriage. As I stirred, Maeyve looked down at me with a sad smile.

*Good morning, beautiful. We're almost there. I hope you slept well.* Maeyve said in my thoughts.

"Why must you use that instead of speaking out loud?" I said hoarsely.

Maeyve laughed lightly as she explained, "In my fox form, I'm able to communicate telepathically with those I am close to, like my family. It's kind of just something I'm used to."

"That makes a lot of sense." As I sat up, I reached for our water bottle and looked out the window.

A few miles out, I could see the castle and bits of the small city on the other side. It was just as Momma had described so many years before. The castle's white and gray stones stood out from the black stones and woods of the other homes I could see. The one-hundred-foot-tall walls were covered in guards protecting the castle and making their rounds. The four cobalt blue-tipped spires were mere feet from the low-hanging white clouds of this world.

The first part of the city we encountered was the homes the townspeople inhabited. The closer we got to the castle, the nicer the houses were. Many of the first homes we passed were dilapidated wooden structures, while the last homes we encountered were similar to Calliope's. The black stone structures were almost three times the size of the previous deteriorated wooden houses.

Next was the market and shops Momma told us about. People of all races and social status meandered about the area. To one side of the street was row upon row of stalls selling fruits, vegetables, meat, fish, and other food items. On the other side were established shops dedicated to clothing, art, and trinkets.

After the luxurious homes and shops, we approached the castle walls. Surrounding them was a moat, similar to the medieval castles I'd heard stories about growing up. I'd seen pictures of medieval castles in the human realm, but they were nowhere near as beautiful as the one before me. Guards stopped the carriage as we approached the bridge leading to the castle gates. Maeyve retrieved our belongings and opened the door, exiting first and then extending her hand to help me down.

With both feet firmly planted on the ground, I stood in awe of the building before me. The castle walls were the tallest structure I'd ever seen. In order to look to the top, I had to lean my head all the way back. The gate ahead was made of the beautiful reddish-brown wood of the trees from the nearby forest and stood at least fifty feet tall.

Five guards stood at the center of the bridge, staring at us. "You smell of the human realm. How the hell did you get here, and what the fuck do you want?" One of the five guards demanded.

Stepping forward with confidence I didn't know I had, I stated, "My name is Anevae, daughter of Princess Cordilaen and granddaughter of King Casimir. I request an audience with the king."

The guards began laughing, but the doors creaked open behind them, and another guard came out. He was tall, beautiful, and dressed in all black with tanned skin. His bright red, round eyes met mine, and a grin spread across his full lips, showing his bright white teeth. When he saw Maeyve standing beside me, his elongated canines almost pierced his bottom lip, deepening his smile.

He clapped and huffed, "Great performance, Anevae. I'm surprised to see that you're here so quickly. Looks like your pet listened and was able to get you here. Come now. Let's get inside. Your grandfather will be pleased to hear of your arrival."

His voice gave him away; *he* was Emrhys. My heart started pounding as I stepped into his space.

I jabbed a finger into his chest and spoke through gritted teeth, "Take me to my grandfather. Now. I want my sister to be released and to return home as soon as possible."

Laughing, he grabbed my hand, and I felt a tingling sensation similar to the one I got when Maeyve touched me. I gasped and pulled away as his mouth popped open.

"What the hell did you just do?" I demanded.

Emrhys recovered quickly and gave me a sinister smile, coming as close as he could without touching me. He leaned down and whispered, "It seems fate has been cruel to us. I never thought I'd find my fated mate, but here we are. It's too bad I'll never be able to mate with you. You're a beautiful and feisty woman, just like I like." He turned on his heel and strolled through the castle gates.

I stood stunned, my mouth hanging open.

Maeyve approached me and asked, "What the hell did he say to you?"

Looking directly into Maeyve's eyes, I asked, "What are fated mates?"

Shocked by my question, Maeyve stammered, "Um, w-well. They're beings destined to be together. Why?"

"Are we fated mates?" I inquired.

Maeyve gave a short laugh and urged me forward, "The fact that we could mark each other and the tingling I feel every time we touch has me thinking that we could be. I was taught very little about any type of mates during my time in Maiviraea. I never thought it was real; I just assumed it was a fairytale."

As I began walking, I asked, "Can a being have more than one fated mate?"

Maeyve abruptly stopped and stared at me. "What did he *actually* say to you, Anevae?"

"He claimed that he and I are fated mates," I murmured.

Maeyve began walking again with her shoulders tensed and her brow furrowed. As we caught up to Emrhys' slow stride, he chuckled deeply.

"Shut the fuck up," I demanded, irritated and confused.

Emrhys ignored my outburst. "I've already sent notice to King Casimir and your sister that you have arrived. They will join us in the throne room shortly."

From there, we walked in silence. After what felt like an eternity and an insane number of turns through the castle, we came to a long hallway with ornate doors at the end. As we approached the doors, the guards who led us opened them. Inside was a room so grand I stopped to stare in awe. The room was made of white marble from top to bottom, and numerous columns lined the walkway to the dias.

Straight ahead of us in the center of the raised dias was a large throne made of dark metal with three spires raised from the back, all tipped with the same cobalt blue stone as the spires on the castle. An orletaylaer, carved in wood and painted the perfect teal color to match the actual flower, was situated below the middle spire—just above the man sitting on the throne. He was a man of tall stature with long, straight black hair and bright yellow eyes. Momma looked nothing like him, but his posture and smugness screamed power. He was my grandfather.

To the left was another large throne decorated almost the same as the other, which was likely meant for the queen. When we saw Calli, she said the queen had been deceased for quite some time, so I wasn't surprised to see that the throne was unoccupied.

Looking to my grandfather's right, I spotted a familiar figure seated on a smaller, less intricate throne, most likely meant for a prince or princess.

"It's nice to see you, Vay."

# About the author

Mikaelynn Rose is a hard-working, devoted mom to an amazing little boy who is her whole world. She is also married to her high school sweetheart. Mikaelynn and her family live near Denver, CO, but she'd much rather be in the country or the mountains. She enjoys coffee, books of many kinds, music, adventuring with her family, and talking to her friends.

Find me on my socials!

facebook.com/mikaelynnrose/

tiktok.com/@mikaelynnrose

tiktok.com/@author.mikaelynn.rose

instagram.com/mikaelynnrose

goodreads.com/mikaelynnrose